"You have great h...
"Very gr...

Maddie looked embarrassed but pleased with his unexpected praise. "Must be the only perk of being a giant."

He heard the dissatisfaction in her voice. "You're not a giant. You didn't tower over the guy you came in with."

"Colton? He's the perfect height."

"You met him today, and you've already fallen for him?"

"Well, when I met him, my heart did do this funny thing."

Dan resisted the temptation to roll his eyes. "Define 'funny thing.'"

She shrugged. "First my chest felt kind of tight, and then my heart raced."

"I don't think that means love. I think it means arrhythmia." He grinned. "So, you think this Colton guy has got it for you?"

Maddie snorted. "Not likely. He can't even remember my name."

Dan didn't know why the idea of Colton raining on Maddie's parade bothered him, but it did. A lot. "He'd be lucky to have you," he said softly.

And then Maddie flashed him a smile so rich in emotion, so totally beautiful, he swore he felt *his* heart zing.

Dear Reader,

In this season of giving thanks, there's only one thing as good as gathering with your family around the holiday table—this month's Silhouette Romance titles, where you're sure to find everything on your romantic wish list!

Hoping Santa will send you on a trip to sunny climes? Visit the romantic world of La Torchere resort with *Rich Man, Poor Bride* (SR #1742), the second book of the miniseries IN A FAIRY TALE WORLD…. Linda Goodnight brings the magic of matchmaking to life with the tale of a sexy Latino doctor who finds love where he least expects it.

And if you're dreaming of a White Christmas, don't miss Sharon De Vita's *Daddy in the Making* (SR#1743). Here, a love-wary cop and a vivacious single mother find themselves snowbound in Wisconsin. Is that a happily-ever-after waiting for them under the tree?

If you've ever ogled a man in a tool belt, and wanted to make him yours, don't miss *The Bowen Bride* (SR #1744) by Nicole Burnham. This wedding shop owner thinks she'll never wear a bridal gown of her own…until she meets a sexy carpenter and his daughter. Perhaps the next dress she sells will be a perfect fit—for her.

Fill your holiday with laughter, courtesy of a new voice in Silhouette Romance—Nancy Lavo—and her story of a fairy godfather and his charge, in *A Whirlwind…Makeover* (SR #1745). When a celebrity photographer recognizes true beauty beneath this ad exec's bad hair and baggy clothes, he's ready to transform her…but can the armor around his heart withstand the woman she's become?

Here's to having your every holiday wish fulfilled!

Sincerely,

Mavis C. Allen
Associate Senior Editor

Please address questions and book requests to:
Silhouette Reader Service
U.S.: 3010 Walden Ave., P.O. Box 1325, Buffalo, NY 14269
Canadian: P.O. Box 609, Fort Erie, Ont. L2A 5X3

A Whirlwind...
Makeover

NANCY LAVO

SILHOUETTE *Romance*®

Published by Silhouette Books

America's Publisher of Contemporary Romance

To John, for twenty-five years of romance.
Thanks for filling my life with love and laughter.

 SILHOUETTE BOOKS

ISBN 0-373-19745-4

A WHIRLWIND...MAKEOVER

Copyright © 2004 by Nancy Lavo

All rights reserved. Except for use in any review, the reproduction
or utilization of this work in whole or in part in any form by any
electronic, mechanical or other means, now known or hereafter
invented, including xerography, photocopying and recording, or in
any information storage or retrieval system, is forbidden without
the written permission of the editorial office, Silhouette Books,
233 Broadway, New York, NY 10279 U.S.A.

All characters in this book have no existence outside the imagination of
the author and have no relation whatsoever to anyone bearing the same
name or names. They are not even distantly inspired by any individual
known or unknown to the author, and all incidents are pure invention.

This edition published by arrangement with Harlequin Books S.A.

® and TM are trademarks of Harlequin Books S.A., used under license.
Trademarks indicated with ® are registered in the United States Patent
and Trademark Office, the Canadian Trade Marks Office and in other
countries.

Visit Silhouette Books at www.eHarlequin.com

Printed in U.S.A.

NANCY LAVO

Nancy's life is all about the basics: companionship, shelter, sustenance and romance. For companionship she married her college sweetheart and had three lovely children. She finds shelter in a little house beneath the wide open skies of Texas. For sustenance she consumes alarming quantities of chocolate. And for romance she relies on her aforementioned college sweetheart and romance novels. When not indulging in a good book, Nancy can be found penning love stories in which the hero and heroine always live happily ever after.

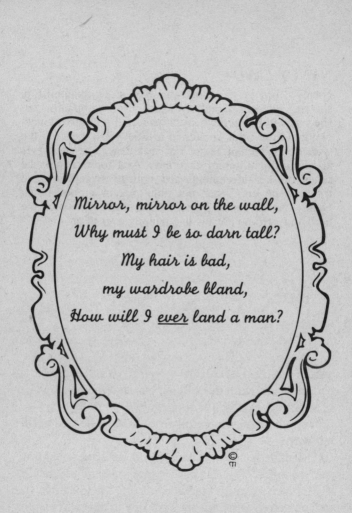

Mirror, mirror on the wall,
Why must I be so darn tall?
My hair is bad,
my wardrobe bland,
How will I _ever_ land a man?

Chapter One

The man was a god.

Not with a capital G of course, but unquestionably one of the Almighty's finest creations. Maddie figured that if angels walked the earth, they would look like this guy: tall and muscular with thick blond hair and the broadest pair of shoulders this side of heaven.

Yup, the man was a god all right. And he was headed her way.

"Maddie, let me introduce you to our newest addition," said her boss. "Colton Hartley, meet Maddie Sinclair."

Her face froze. Her mouth went dry. Maddie forced her tongue across her suddenly stiff lips in hopes of coaxing them to smile.

"Nice to meet you, Colton." Her normally low voice sounded lower still and her greeting was the scratchy croak of a groggy bullfrog.

He didn't seem to notice. He smiled, a perfect tooth-paste-ad smile, and Maddie felt the room brighten and the temperature soar. Her heart did a flip-flop. He extended his hand. "Great to meet you."

She shook his hand. Too late she realized where all the moisture from her mouth had gone. Her hand practically dripped clammy sweat. Colton was too much a gentleman to wipe his hands on his slacks.

"Maddie," her boss, Jack Benson, was saying, "it'll take Colton a while to learn the ropes around here. I wondered if you'd be willing to act as his guide for the next couple of days. To make certain he settles in."

She nodded. "Sure." Willing? Major understatement. She was willing all right. To be his guide, his slave, the mother of his children. Whatever.

She was so willing that her head continued to bob the affirmative like one of those tacky ceramic dogs people put in the rear windows of their cars.

Time to get a grip on herself. After all, Colton Hartley was only a man, albeit a perfect specimen. She stilled her bobbing head and smiled. "I'd be happy to help."

Jack grinned. "Great. I've got some stuff I need to get done this morning, so I'll let you take over from here." He clapped Colton on the shoulder. "I'm leaving you in good hands."

Jack winked at Maddie behind Colton's back and walked away.

Bless Jack's devious heart. He was always trying to jump-start her social life. Correction. To jump-start her social life would require that she had one. Which she did not. Yet.

"Where to first?" she asked Colton. "What have you al-ready seen?"

"Nothing. You were the first stop on the tour."

Double blessings on Jack. "Then we'll start at the front door. Let me introduce you to our receptionist."

It was encouraging to know that Maddie wasn't the only one stricken with idiocy when face-to-face with Colton. Crystal, the cute little blond receptionist, was clearly awed.

"Wow," she said in a breathless voice after Maddie had performed the introductions. "Wow."

"Nice to meet you, Crystal."

Crystal wasn't quite the clod Maddie had been. She was stunned, but not so shaken that she forgot the basics of flirtation. Easily a foot shorter than Colton, she lowered her chin to look up through her eyelashes at him.

Nice trick, Maddie thought. She wouldn't be opposed to trying it herself, but at five-eleven there were precious few men she could look up at.

"Welcome to Cue Communications," Crystal purred.

Maddie saw his smile widen in appreciation and two dimples appeared in his chiseled cheeks. Uh-oh. Afraid she'd lose him before she'd won him, Maddie hustled Colton along to the second point on the tour.

A familiar sense of pride filled her as she led him down the plush gray-carpeted hall. Cue Communications, with its sleek Art Deco décor was the top advertising agency in the Dallas-Fort Worth metroplex. Once a dining-room-table enterprise of two visionary young men, Cue now comprised the entire thirty-second floor of the prestigious Tower Building in downtown Fort Worth.

"This is the graphics department. Nick Hodges is our art director."

Nick stepped away from the table where he was constructing a storyboard. "Hi. What can I do for you?"

Colton stuck out his hand. "Colton Hartley. I just signed on with Cue. Molly here is showing me around."

"Maddie," she corrected.

"Right. Maddie," he said, with the briefest glance toward her.

Nick and Colton spoke for a few minutes about advertising and music and football. Maddie couldn't tell by the conversation whether Colton knew what he was talking about, but it was obvious he was a natural schmoozer. He had Nick eating out of his hand in no time.

"I'll let you get back to work, Nick. Molly and I should continue on the grand tour."

"It's Maddie," she said.

He looked startled, then apologetic. "Sure. Sorry. See ya around, Nick."

Maddie took him to the big conference room at the far end of the hall where they held staff functions and important client meetings. She took him to the production rooms and introduced him to the people on the creative team.

Wherever they went the response was the same. Colton Hartley knocked them dead. Every square inch of his perfect six-foot-three-inch frame oozed charisma. He had only to smile at the ladies and talk sports with the men, and they were putty in his well-manicured hands. If the man ever decided to try his hand at politics, no office in the land would be out of his reach.

Even more amazing than his power over humankind was the fact that he was currently assigned to Maddie's care. Maddie could hardly believe her luck. The couple of days they would have together while he became acclimated to the firm would surely give her the inside track. Working side by side, he'd recognize her charm and intelligence and fall under her as-yet-undiscovered spell.

Whoa, girl. Maddie mentally halted her galloping imagination before she had them married with two kids, a dog and a mortgage.

First things first. She had to get him away from the crowd currently fluttering around him like moths to a porch light so she could get in some quality one-on-one time with him.

"I think you've seen all the highlights," Maddie said. "Are you ready to head back to your office?"

Colton looked up from his throng of admirers. "Sure."

Colton had been given one of the coveted offices with a window overlooking downtown Fort Worth. Unlike Maddie's cramped office with scarcely enough room for a desk and credenza, Colton's office was furnished with a large desk, two credenzas and a cozy grouping of two high-back leather chairs separated by a small round table.

As Colton sat at his desk, sunlight streamed through the window to bathe him with a golden aura. Maddie scooted one of the heavy chairs up close to his desk and sat. She allowed herself a moment to admire his now-radiant beauty before getting started.

"I don't know if Jack spoke with you about our current bid to retain the Swanson Shoes account?"

Colton smiled and lifted the manila folder from the center of his desk. "We discussed it briefly. He gave me this file to review."

"Oh." Drat. She'd wanted to be the one to introduce him to the situation. To dazzle him with her insight.

Colton flipped open the file and began to read.

Maddie shifted forward to rest her elbows on the desktop and propped her chin in her hands to watch. He was magnificent. His heavily lashed blue eyes darted across the typed notes. As he turned the page he reached a long-fingered hand to his mouth. When he absently stroked his lower lip with his fingertip, Maddie sighed.

Colton looked up as if surprised she was still there. "Don't let me keep you," he said. "I've got it from here."

Her heart sank. "Are you sure?"

He nodded and stood. "This report seems pretty thorough. I'll call you if I have any questions."

She couldn't very well stay after he'd so obviously dismissed her. She stood. "If you're sure..."

He smiled. "I think I can handle it." He walked around the desk and placed a warm hand on her shoulder. "Thanks for this morning's tour, Mandy. I really appreciated it."

She didn't correct him. She couldn't. She could hardly breathe. Not when he was smiling as though she was the most important person in the world.

Dazed, she moved toward the door. Before exiting, she paused to say, "I'll come by your office about noon to show you where everybody goes for lunch."

He'd already reseated himself and was studying the report. He didn't look up. "Fine."

Maddie floated to her office and closed the door to daydream in privacy. There was no way she could concentrate on the Swanson Shoes account when she had a lunch date with the most beautiful man in the world.

At 11:45 a.m. Maddie grabbed her purse from the bottom drawer of her file cabinet and headed to the ladies' room for a little prelunch primping. Her conscience nagged her about quitting work so early, but she silenced it with the knowledge that she hadn't accomplished anything all morning anyway. Who could concentrate on clients when the man of her dreams occupied the office three doors down?

She had the elegant gold-and-ivory powder room to herself. She stopped in front of the first sink under the lighted wall-long mirror and got started. From the large black leather tote bag that did double duty as her purse she pulled out a toothbrush and tube of toothpaste. After a thorough scrubbing she gargled a mouthful of the mouthwash she carried for emergencies.

As she rinsed the residue down the drain she studied her reflection. For a change, her long curly hair hadn't escaped the two dozen pins and half bottle of hair spray that secured it to her head. It didn't look great, but it was neat, so she opted to leave it alone.

She wasn't a big makeup enthusiast so all that was left was to reapply her lipstick. She carefully filled in her upper and lower lip with the tube of rosy-pink gloss she found wedged in the bottom corner of her bag. She smacked her lips together and stepped back from the mirror to get the full effect.

Hmm. No point in kidding herself. Miss America she wasn't. Unlike her five-foot-three-inch blond sister, who'd had the good sense to take after their beautiful petite mother, Maddie was the spitting image of her dad.

Her smile faded. Though he'd been gone five years now, the still-sharp pain of losing him brought tears to her eyes.

Her dad had been a great big teddy bear—the classic gentle giant. He had stood an impressive six and a half feet tall and weighed in at 290 pounds. Though his size had certainly attracted attention, it was his kind heart and easy-going nature that had endeared him to everyone.

Maddie liked to think she'd inherited his character traits—his incurable optimism and ability to see beyond the surface to the beauty beneath—but she fervently wished that she'd physically favored her mom.

Inner beauty was a fine thing, but it was external beauty that snared the men. It was great to have people say she was the nicest person they knew, but she'd cheerfully forgo the compliment just once for an honest-to-goodness date.

Maddie returned her gaze to her reflection and purposely stretched her mouth into a wide smile. She had a date now—in a manner of speaking. Colton Hartley, advertising executive extraordinaire, was hers for the next hour.

They didn't have much time. She needed to strategize to make the most of every minute. She'd take him down to the cafeteria on the lobby level. They'd sit at one of the small square tables that lined the far wall of the room. Preferably one tucked behind a potted plant.

She closed her eyes to complete the fairy tale. Without the distractions of fellow employees, they'd talk about themselves and the incredible good fortune that had brought them together. Colton's beautiful blue eyes would look into hers and he would see her as no one had seen her since her father had been alive. As a rare treasure worthy of love.

Maddie's heart hammered against her ribs as she reached up to knock on Colton's door.

"Come in."

Maddie took two steps into the room that now smelled faintly of his cologne. "Ready to eat?"

He looked up from the notes he was making in the Swanson file. He smiled, his perfect teeth blindingly white against his tan. "You bet."

He was even better looking than she remembered. She stifled a sigh. "Great. Let's go."

It took nearly ten minutes to make the five-second walk to the elevator. It couldn't be coincidence that every female employee, and a few males, just happened to pop out of their offices at the exact moment she and Colton passed. Though she couldn't avoid stopping and chatting half a dozen times, she refused to lose sight of her objective. Colton was hers and hers alone for the next hour.

She could have wept with relief when the elevator doors whispered shut on just the two of them.

"Cue Communications is such a friendly place," Colton said as Maddie pushed the down button.

The man had a gift for understatement. Co-workers mobbed him like groupies around a rock star. "So I've noticed."

He inclined his head to her and smiled. "I appreciate you going to the trouble of showing me around, though I'm sure I could have found the cafeteria on my own."

"No way."

Colton's eyes widened a fraction at the steel in her voice.

She tried for the lowered-chin, look-up-through-the-eyelashes approach. "What I mean is, there's no way I'd desert you on your first day. I've got Cue's friendly reputation to live up to."

His face relaxed into a heart-stopping smile. "That's real nice."

The elevator doors opened onto the lobby, now

crammed with people. Darn. She shouldn't have waited till straight-up noon to take him to lunch. The cafeteria served good food and was a real favorite with the office-building crowd. They were all here today.

Maddie and Colton fell into the lineup of about twenty people waiting to pick up trays and make selections. She did some hasty calculations. At the rate things were moving they'd have only forty-five minutes sequestered at their table. Only a fool would waste these precious moments in line. And her daddy didn't raise no fool.

"So, Colton," she began. "How did you end up at Cue?"

A cute, size-four redhead standing two people in front of them turned at the sound of his name. "Colton? Colton Hartley?"

His handsome face lit up in recognition. "Paige?"

Their warm reunion carried them all the way to the tray and silverware pickup.

"It's great seeing you, Paige," Colton said as he pocketed the slip of paper she'd handed him with her phone number on it. "I'll give you a call and we can get together."

Maddie didn't allow her heart to sink. After all, a man like Colton Hartley didn't reach this stage in his gorgeous life without acquiring a few female friends. Just because their greeting seemed a tad overwarm to Maddie didn't guarantee that Paige meant anything to him.

"So what's good?" he asked Maddie, the first time he'd spoken to her since her brief introduction to the red-haired interloper.

"Everything." Maddie had her eye on the warming tray stacked high with crispy chicken-fried steaks. Yum. A glob of mashed potatoes and cream gravy alongside would make the perfect lunch.

Colton looked down the length of the serving island, considering the options before picking up a chef's salad and plunking it down on his tray.

"Is that all you're having?" Maddie asked as they inched their way toward the golden chicken-fried steaks and steaming gravy.

"Yeah." He motioned toward the steaks and delicacies beyond. "If you eat all that heavy stuff for lunch it doesn't take long before the pounds start adding up." He patted his rock-hard stomach for emphasis.

Maddie thought about her own not-so-rock-hard stomach and suddenly the chicken-fried steak didn't look so good. She snatched up a green salad and a paper container of diet dressing instead. She sped by the freshly baked pies before temptation could destroy her fragile newfound willpower.

After paying the cashier for their food, Colton and Maddie paused to scout the crowded room for a table.

"I think I see a table over there," Maddie said, pointing to the far wall. She squinted to be sure. "Can you see it behind the palm?"

"Lead the way."

Trays in hand, they forged a path through the occupied tables.

"Hey, Colton, over here." A preppie-looking guy waved at them from his table some ten yards away.

"Okay with you?" Colton asked, lifting a muscular shoulder in the direction of the caller.

Her heart slipped a few notches. "Sure."

With Colton now leading, they threaded their way to the table, trays lifted high to keep from bumping into diners. Maddie hung back to allow Colton time to make introductions.

"Good to see you, Colton." The preppie clapped Colton on the back. "What brings you to our little corner of the world?"

The predominately female group seated around the rectangular table greeted Colton like a visiting celebrity. Or a god. A woman skinny enough to shop in the preteen department patted the empty seat next to hers. "Come sit here."

While they fussed over Colton, Maddie did the math. One preppie, one accountant type, five skinny hussies and one delectable Colton. Eight bodies. Table for eight.

There wasn't room for her.

Maddie stood several inconspicuous steps from the table, waiting for Colton to notice her predicament. Once he saw she was still standing he'd insist they drag an extra chair up to the table for her.

She waited.

When one minute had lapsed into two and he still hadn't looked up from his friends, Maddie knew she'd been forgotten. She couldn't blame him. Who wouldn't forget their own name in the midst of all that adulation?

Not wanting to embarrass him or herself, Maddie backed up in retreat. As she slowly moved backward, a stupid smile plastered on her face, Maddie didn't notice the abandoned chair blocking the aisle. Inching along, her leg caught the chair rung and she knew in that awful moment that to cap off her humiliation, she was going to fall.

"Whoa." A deep voice rumbled in her ear as strong arms came from behind to steady her.

Her heart seemed to stop. Her stomach did a long, slow slide. It took Maddie a second or two to realize the hideous downward pull of gravity had been broken. She wasn't going to fall. She'd been saved.

Balance restored, Maddie turned, tray in hand, to thank her rescuer.

Dark eyes, the color of the richest chocolate and tinged with amusement, met hers. "You okay?" he asked.

Chapter Two

"I'm fine, thanks to you." Obviously shaken by her near fall, the woman's pleasantly husky voice wobbled. "I'm not usually so clumsy. I guess I wasn't watching where I was going."

Dan had seen her slow progress through the crowded room and knew full well why she'd stumbled. She was one-hundred-percent focused on the movie-star guy she'd come in with. As was half the population of the room. "No problem. You want to sit down?" he asked, pointing to the chair that had nearly toppled her. "I've got room for you here."

After an almost imperceptible glance toward the movie star's table, she turned to Dan and smiled. "Thanks."

She had a great smile. Full. Warm. Sincere.

And a really great mouth. Full. Warm. Delicious. He knew the camera would love it, though at the moment his thoughts weren't entirely professional.

Dan eased the tray from her white-knuckled grip and placed it on the table before maneuvering the chair from the aisle. He waited until she sat down before sitting across from her.

"I'm Dan Willis."

She smiled again. "Maddie Sinclair," she said, extending her hand to him.

"Nice to meet you, Maddie." He glanced down at the puny salad on her tray. "Not much lunch."

She looked at the red plastic bowl half filled with greens and wrinkled her nose. "No."

He tapped the dessert plate on the edge of his tray. "Tell you what. You eat all your salad and I'll give you a bite of my pie."

She grinned. "Deal."

Dan watched her pour the watery dressing over the lettuce and pick up her fork. "Great hands," he said.

Her fork froze, drippy lettuce dangling in midair. "I'm sorry?"

"I said you have great hands. Very graceful. You have the perfect combination of slender palms and long fingers."

She looked embarrassed but pleased with the unexpected praise. "Long fingers must be the only perk of being a giant."

He heard the dissatisfaction in her voice. "You're not a giant. You're tall. What are you, six feet?"

"Only five-eleven," she corrected in a way that told him that that one inch was important to her.

"If I look taller it's the hair," she continued while pointing to what looked like an ugly brown badger hibernating on top of her head. "It's long and thick. I pin it up on the top of my head to keep it out of the way. Once I tried pinning it around the sides of my head, but it looked like I was wearing a hairy inner-tube crown. I probably look taller with it pinned up this way, but really I'm only five-eleven."

"I believe you." He took a bite of his sandwich. "I take it you don't like being tall."

She blew out a frustrated breath. "I hate it. Trust me, it's only in fairy tales that giants have the advantage. In real life we have to buy ugly flat shoes and slump our shoulders to keep from towering over everyone."

"You didn't seem to tower over the guy you came in with."

"Colton?" Her gaze traveled to the movie star's table and her expression softened. "He's the perfect height."

"Perfect for what?"

Her eyes remained trained on Colton. "For me."

"He's *your* guy?" Dan hoped his astonishment didn't bleed through to his voice.

She dragged her eyes back to Dan. "No," she admitted with an embarrassed blush.

Dan sensed there was an interesting story here. "How do you know him?"

She leaned in, eager to talk about Colton. "We work together. At Cue Communications. He just came on board today."

"You met him today, and you've already fallen for him?"

"Sounds crazy, doesn't it? I'm not usually the impulsive type. I don't even believe in love at first sight. Or didn't. There's just something about Colton."

He couldn't keep the cynicism from his tone. "Mind if I hazard a guess? Could it be that he looks like a movie star?"

She dismissed the idea with a graceful wave of her hand. "Oh no. I mean, sure, he's fabulous looking, but there's more to it than that."

"Like what?"

She hesitated. "Promise you won't laugh?"

He hadn't been tempted to until he saw her suddenly solemn expression. He chewed the insides of his mouth. "I promise."

"My dad always told me that when I met Mr. Right, he'd knock me off my feet. Not literally, of course. He used to say that when he met my mom his heart went zing and he knew she was the one. It happened to me today. The minute I saw Colton my heart did this funny thing."

Dan resisted the temptation to roll his eyes. "Define 'funny thing.'"

She shrugged. "I can't explain it exactly. It was a weird feeling. First my chest felt kind of tight, and then my heart raced."

Dan swallowed his last bite of sandwich. "I don't think a tight chest and a racing heart mean love. I think it means arrhythmia. Could be deadly. You probably ought to have it checked out."

She laughed. "You're obviously not a romantic."

"Obviously not." Dan scooted the plate of pie between them. "Time for dessert. Eat up."

She didn't need a second invitation. Seemed the tiny salad hadn't filled her up. She and Dan talked and laughed as they demolished the pie.

"So, you think this Colton guy has got it for you? Think his heart zinged?"

Maddie snorted. "Not likely. He can't even remember my name. Kept calling me Molly or Mandy."

Ouch. Dan wasn't surprised to hear Maddie didn't turn the golden boy's head. Guys like Colton went for bombshells, not bombs. And the shapeless black dress and *Wild Kingdom* hairdo Maddie wore were bonafide bombs. Still, Dan felt an urge to soften the blow. "Don't be discouraged. He probably had a lot of distractions, this being his first day and all."

"He had a lot of distractions all right—short, skinny female ones." She lifted her chin a fraction. "But I'm not discouraged. I hope that after he gets to know me he'll see that I have some great qualities. It's the inside that counts."

That had to be the bravest speech he'd ever heard. And the dumbest. Old Colton didn't look like the type to seek out great qualities. Fact was he didn't look the type to see beyond his own mirror.

Dan didn't know why the idea of Colton raining on Maddie's parade bothered him, but it did. It was obvious her self-esteem was already at rock bottom. He hated to think what the inevitable rejection would do to her. "He'd be lucky to have you."

She flashed him a smile so rich in emotion, so totally beautiful he swore he felt *his* heart zing. "Thanks."

She glanced down at her watch then picked up her purse—a hideous, scarred black leather bag large enough to carry a week's worth of clothing. She stood. "I need to get back to the office."

Dan stood. "It was nice meeting you."

"I had fun," Maddie said. "And thanks for the pie." She grinned. "I believe there was enough chocolate in it to tide me over till my candy-bar break at three."

She turned and took two steps from the table before stopping and turning back. She lowered her voice so no one at the surrounding tables could hear her. "What you said earlier, about my hands being great—that was really nice. Thanks."

Dan unlocked the door to his office and stepped inside just as the phone rang. He crossed to the desk, a strictly utilitarian steel model he'd picked up in a secondhand office furniture store, pressed the flashing button on the phone and picked up the receiver. "This is Dan."

"Dan, ol' buddy. Ryan here. I called to see if you'd had enough of the wilds of Texas? Are you ready to return to civilization?"

Dan settled back into his swivel chair and propped his cowboy-booted heels on top of the desk. He chuckled. "Not a chance."

"Come on, man. You've been there, what, two weeks now? Surely that's enough time for you to come to your senses."

"I have come to my senses. That's why I'm back in Texas."

Ryan's tone changed from teasing to lecturing. "I know you think you're burned out, but you're not. You have an incredibly successful career up here. People do not burn out on incredibly successful careers. Besides, you love New York. Everybody loves New York."

"You're right. I love New York. But I needed a break. I needed to get away."

"Fine. Take another week. Then get on a plane. There's a big shoot in Milan in two weeks. We'll do it together."

"No can do."

"Why not? What are you going to do buried down there?"

"I don't know. I'm not sure yet."

"Okay. I won't press you." Ryan paused. "So, tell me, are the women down there as beautiful as you remembered?"

Dan smiled. Before he'd packed up and moved back to Texas Dan had bragged that Texan women were the most beautiful in the world. And he'd meant it. He couldn't think of another group of women anywhere in the world who invested the kind of time and effort in themselves that Texan women did. Young or old, fat or skinny, it was as though they had an innate understanding of their worth.

Except Maddie.

Five feet and eleven inches—four inches of badger hair not withstanding—Maddie didn't seem to have that Texas confidence. If anything, she undervalued herself.

Instead of carrying her commanding height with pride, she rolled her shoulders forward as if trying to shrink from sight. He couldn't tell if she had a figure: no body, no matter how bad, deserved to be draped in the long, flowy black thing she'd been wearing today. It looked more like a bad slipcover than a dress. The meager attention she gave her hair and makeup said she didn't see the point in trying. She felt she was hopeless.

Dan's practiced eye told him nothing could be farther from the truth. If you could get past the thick black eyebrows that were separated by a scant half inch of flesh, Maddie had an excellent forehead, well-defined cheekbones, and a strong but feminine nose. She had a mile-wide smile with straight white teeth and the full lower lip that women were willing to suffer collagen injections to achieve.

The memory of Maddie's mouth made *his* mouth water.

How many times had he forced his focus away from her lips so he could concentrate on what she was saying?

Maddie had all the right stuff. And so much more.

Years of working with the world's most acclaimed beauties had taught him that good physical attributes rarely added up to true beauty. More often they equaled cold hauteur and empty vanity, women who would cheerfully spend an evening with only a mirror for company.

He'd gotten to the point recently, when looking through the camera lens, that he couldn't find the shot he wanted because he couldn't find the beauty. His last shoot ran a record nine hours. The fault hadn't been a temperamental model. It had been him.

He'd become cynical and he knew it. And when the cynicism became debilitating he'd packed up his camera and walked away. He was tired of looking for beauty where it didn't exist. So he'd come home.

Funny that his first glimpse of beauty should be in the most unlikely person. In the short time he'd spent with Maddie he'd seen something he'd begun to doubt existed. A beauty that transcended good bones.

Of course, first impressions could be deceiving. Beneath her refreshing openness could be an empty shell like that he'd seen in so many others.

Maddie Sinclair intrigued him. He'd just have to get a second impression to find out.

"Are they as beautiful as I remembered?" Dan said, repeating his friend's question. "Let me get back to you on that."

Chapter Three

Maddie picked up her yellow legal pad and freshly sharpened pencil and walked to the door of her office. She'd left it slightly ajar so she could see when Colton started down the hall for the Monday morning staff meeting.

She assured her troublesome conscience that she was not stalking the man—she simply wanted to be handy if he needed reassurance during the first difficult days of his new job. Not that she honestly believed he'd ever suffered even a moment of self-doubt in his gorgeous life. Whereas mere mortals were composed of ninety-something percent water, Colton Hartley was pure unadulterated confidence.

Maddie knew her own confidence level frequently dipped into the non-existent range. That's probably one of the myriad reasons she found Colton Hartley so attractive. He was everything she was not.

She had hoped to serve as his guide over the next few days, but unfortunately he'd made it very clear last Friday afternoon when she'd walked him out to his car at the end of the day that he no longer required her services. His exact words were, "You've done a great job of showing me around, Maddie, but I can handle it from here."

Despite her protests, he was determined to go it alone. Though deprived of a valid excuse to stick by his side, she was pleased he'd finally remembered her name.

And though he was determined to stand on his own two feet, she was equally determined to stand by his side. And anyone who knew Maddie at all knew that what she lacked in self-confidence she more than made up for in sheer determination.

So here she was, lurking in the doorway, eye pressed to the crack so he couldn't slip by. Lucky for her his office was on the opposite side of the hall: if she stood at just the right angle to the opening she could see his office door.

Moving shadows alerted her that he was finally coming out. When she saw his broad shoulders fill his doorway she counted three seconds before swinging open her door and stepping out into the hall. She knew immediately the delay had been a mistake. Even as she moved in on his retreating form, people were popping out of their offices like cuckoos from a clock just as Colton passed by.

Coincidence? Maddie doubted it. She began to suspect hers had not been the only eye pressed to a door crack that morning.

She hurried, trying to catch up with Colton's long-legged stride, but it was no use. Her female colleagues had already closed in on him.

She resisted the temptation to gnash her teeth. There would be other times.

Maddie filed into the conference room with the others. The seats around the long mahogany table were already taken so she settled into one of the chairs set up in the back of the room.

Less than five minutes later Jack Benson, owner of Cue Communications, called the meeting to order. Jack and Maddie's late father had started Cue Communications thirty years ago. At the time, they'd had one client and no prospects. The only thing the two young men had had in abundance was ambition.

Through grit and perseverance they'd built the advertising agency into a well-respected firm billing millions in revenue annually. The staff had grown to eighteen full-time employees and their client list read like a Who's Who of the Dallas-Fort Worth area.

As a little girl, Maddie's heart's desire had been to work side by side with her father at Cue. When he'd died unexpectedly before she'd graduated from college, Jack had assured her she'd always have a place at the agency. A year after her dad had died, her mother sold Jack their half of the agency, preferring the lucrative cash settlement to the messy details of owning a business. Though Maddie no longer held physical ownership of the company, in her heart it would always be hers and her dad's.

She'd hired on a year ago, after earning her MBA, with the nebulous title of Jack's assistant. She didn't have the experience required of an account executive, nor the talent for art or copywriting, but she had drive. Jack had signed her on with a handsome salary and an office of her own.

She'd never forget the day he'd first introduced her at the Monday morning meeting. She'd sat beside him at the head of the table, and, when it came time for introductions, they stood, his arm around her shoulders, and he had said to the assembled staff, "You are looking at the brightest star on the horizon of Cue Communications."

She wasn't sure why, but he believed in her. Other than her father, Jack was the only one who thought she was bright, capable and creative.

Jack had spent the past year training her. He'd taught her about the fine art of marketing and forecasting trends. He'd showed her the production side of the business, so she knew firsthand how a concept evolved into a storyboard and finally into a finished campaign. More importantly, he'd modeled the integrity and ambition she'd admired in her father.

Maddie desperately wanted to live up to the potential Jack saw in her. As his assistant she listened carefully, absorbing the information he'd given her. But after a year, she still kept to the background. When Jack questioned her as to why she didn't share her ideas with the group, she told him honestly that she didn't feel she'd earned the right to speak. What were her opinions compared to those with years of experience?

The sound of laughter dragged her attention to the present. As always, Jack had opened the meeting with a joke. When the laughter died down, he officially introduced Colton to the group. Maddie didn't miss the particularly warm reception the women gave him. Colton accepted it graciously, said a few words of greeting and sat down.

"Now, on to the business at hand," Jack said. "I received a call from Swanson Shoes last week. Old man

Swanson is stepping down from leadership and his son Paul is taking his place. Swanson wanted me to know that Paul is considering dropping Cue and going with a new agency."

Jack paused while a worried buzz filled the room. "Paul thinks Swanson Shoes needs new blood to freshen up the company image. In deference to our long-standing friendship, Swanson has requested that Paul give us the opportunity to pitch a new campaign before he makes any changes. Paul agreed. I set a tentative meeting for Friday."

The buzz became a roar.

Jack held up his hand for silence. "I know that doesn't give us much time, but I believe the faster we get back to him, the more likely we are to retain the account. Once the news gets out that Swanson Shoes is up for grabs, agencies will swarm them. I don't have to tell you that nobody wins in a frenzied bidding war."

Again he lifted his hands in a call to order. "I'm personally going to handle the new pitch and I'm going to ask Colton to work with me."

Colton smiled and nodded his acceptance to Jack, obviously pleased with the honor.

"And Maddie, I'm looking for your input as well."

She'd known when Jack had given her the information last week that he wanted her opinion of the situation, but she'd never dreamed he wanted her on the account team. Though her stomach lurched with the weight of the responsibility, she, too, gave Jack a calm nod.

The rest of the meeting passed in a blur. Maddie couldn't muster any enthusiasm for the current cheap toy promotion their hamburger chain was offering. Her mind was locked on the idea that Swanson Shoes, one of their biggest, most lucrative accounts, was in jeopardy and she was on the team to save it. Even the honor of working side by side with Colton was of secondary importance.

After Jack dismissed the meeting, he asked Colton and Maddie, along with the creative team, to stay. Maddie picked up her pad and pencil and relocated to the open chair at Jack's left.

When the room cleared, Jack said, "You both have had an opportunity to study the Swanson account. You've heard me say the new president, a thirty-two-year-old hotshot, is ready to replace us with new blood. What do you think we should do about it?"

He turned to Maddie. "Ladies first."

She'd had plenty of time to prepare what she wanted to say, but when it came time to speak nerves blocked her throat. "I think—" Her voice was a croak. She swallowed hard and cleared her throat. Twice.

"I think it's time to change the focus of the campaign. For the past twelve years we've sold Swanson Shoes as good value. We've concentrated almost exclusively on the price angle. Last week I researched the price of comparable children's shoes in local stores and found that Swanson Shoes are expensive. I don't have the exact numbers with me but Swanson Shoes are typically priced thirty percent higher than their competitors' shoes."

Jack nodded and made a little humming sound of approval.

Maddie continued with more confidence, careful to avoid looking at Colton so she wouldn't get distracted. "I also noticed that while the prices were higher, so was the quality. Swanson Shoes were superior to every other shoe I compared them to. Through personal observation and questioning the sales people I found that the average Swanson Shoe customer is a double-income couple. I know money is important to everyone, but I think these customers would be motivated to buy a shoe for quality and construction. Even status."

Jack's brows shot up.

"Let's compare it to buying cars. The upwardly mobile rarely drive economy cars even though they provide adequate transportation. No, they buy luxury cars because they want the status. They don't mind paying the bigger price tag because they believe they are getting more. The finest quality. Exclusivity." Maddie took a deep breath before finishing, "Bottom line, I think we should sell Swanson Shoes like Cadillacs. We would use the angle that their children deserve the best."

Jack's grin nearly split his face. He looked so proud Maddie half expected him to burst the buttons on his shirt.

Colton leaned forward, shaking his head. "I disagree. I think money is always of paramount importance, especially in uncertain economies like ours. I believe we're dead-on by making value the focus of the campaign."

With all attention riveted on him, Colton stood and began to pace. "As I see it, the problem isn't the focus of the campaign, it's the delivery. I took the Swanson Shoe video home over the weekend and watched the current television ads. B-o-r-i-n-g. This new president, Paul, is looking for fresh and innovative ideas. I think what is called for here is flashy presentation. New music, bold colors, aggressive staging. There's nothing wrong with Maddie's ideas, but in execution I believe we'd be giving Swanson Shoes more of the same stuff they've come to expect from Cue. We'd be handing Paul all the excuse he needs to walk."

He was good. Maddie didn't enjoy having her ideas shot down like mallards in duck season, but she had to admit, Colton did it with panache. He paced as he delivered his ideas, stopping and gesturing at dramatic intervals. Between the sight of his impressive self and the ringing authority in his voice, Maddie was half convinced she was an idiot. Evidently so were the others.

The creative team was one hundred percent behind Colton. Jack seemed less certain. He sat back in his black leather chair, balanced his elbows on the tabletop and steepled his fingers. After a lengthy silence he said, "Both ideas have merit…"

Colton seemed to sense his advantage, "Jack, you brought me on to update Cue's image. I hope you'll go with the same instincts that led you to me and allow me to draw up the campaign."

Maddie wanted to applaud. The guy was a master. He seemed to be a natural at reading the crowd and delivering what they wanted. Wouldn't that same innate ability apply to advertising?

Maddie thought her ideas were good. Really good. But what if she was wrong? It's not like she had years of experience behind her. She certainly didn't have Colton's knack for reading people.

It was hard to give up her own plan, which she believed was a sound one, but ultimately the good of Cue outweighed her need for validation and acceptance. "I think he's right, Jack," she said.

Jack turned to study her face and gauge her sincerity. She nodded and smiled her approval. After another long pause Jack said, "Okay, creative people, you've heard Colton's ideas. Flesh them out for me. I want sample print campaigns, radio spots and 30-second television spots. Make them trendy enough to convince Paul Swanson that Cue Communications has not gone the way of the dinosaur."

Colton had a five-minute head start on Maddie when she headed downstairs for lunch. With her eye once again pressed to the door she'd seen him switch off his office light and head down the hall. Forgoing a delay for the sake of appearances, she darted out to follow him.

She'd have caught up with him if Jack hadn't caught her.

"Maddie," he called from his office. "Come in for a second. And close the door."

She had no choice but to obey. She cast one last longing look at Colton's retreating back before entering Jack's office and closing the door behind her. She took the chair across from him at the desk.

Jack's normally jovial expression was serious. "I want you to tell me honestly what you think of Colton's ideas for Swanson's campaign."

She met his eyes to give him the reassurance he sought. "I liked them. You know they're not the direction I'd have originally chosen. I've never been a big fan of loud music and erratic photography to sell a product. However, all that said, I believe Colton will make them work."

She sat forward in her chair to continue. "From the little I've seen of him, I know he's a natural. You've seen him, Jack. He works a crowd like a seasoned politician. If he brings that same power to an ad campaign, I can't see how it could lose."

"He's good all right, but my gut instinct tells me your strategy is better."

Maddie thought those were the nicest words she'd ever heard.

Jack said, "This is going to sound crazy, but the fact that I agree with you is why I decided to go with Colton."

"You're right. It sounds crazy."

"Hear me out. Paul Swanson thinks Cue Communications is outdated. Since I've had the largest input in his previous campaigns I translate that to mean that I'm outdated. I've spent the last year teaching you everything I know. You and I think alike."

Maddie nodded. "I see what you're getting at. It's possible you like my idea because it's a product of your training."

"Exactly. I don't ordinarily second-guess myself. I've been in this business a long time and I have developed a certain sense about what works. But I've got to tell you, I was rattled when old man Swanson told me we were in danger of losing the account. For the first time, I wondered if I've been around too long. If my perspective is stale."

He suddenly looked older. Grayer. Maddie reached across the desk to take his hand in hers. "My dad always said you were an advertising genius. And he was right. Part of that genius led you to Colton. Instinct told you he had something you wanted for Cue. You were right to go with your instincts. He can give Paul something totally new and different. And new and different just might be the ticket."

He squeezed her hand with fatherly affection. "Thanks, Maddie."

"For what?"

"For taking this so well. When I asked you to join the Swanson team I did it because I know your ideas are good and I wanted you to realize it, too. You finally open up and your ideas get shot down. That's not how I planned it. So thanks, for being a big enough person to consider someone else's ideas."

She laughed as she stood. "You know as well as I do that no one has ever accused me of being less than a big person."

His laughter trailed her down the hall.

Maddie once again selected a green salad for lunch. For variation she went with the diet Italian dressing that strongly resembled water with red and green flecks. Just past the cashier she paused to scan the room for Colton. Her first sweep came up empty. She sighed. With so many people milling around she might never locate him.

About halfway through her second sweep she caught sight of someone waving. Her heart skipped a beat until she realized it wasn't Colton. It was Dan, the guy she'd shared a table and a piece of pie with on Friday. She balanced her tray in one hand and waved back before continuing her search for Colton. No sign of him.

Maddie glanced back at Dan. He was standing now, waving her over to his table. She hesitated. She didn't want to commit herself should she suddenly locate Colton. She darted several more fruitless looks around the room.

Finally, good manners propelled her toward Dan. He was kind enough to offer her a seat and, realistically, she might never find Colton. Besides, Dan just might have another piece of pie he was willing to share.

It was slow going through the obstacle course of people and tables. Dan was smiling when at last she reached him. A crinkly eyed smile that made Maddie feel as though she'd stepped into a pool of bright sunlight.

"Hi, Maddie," he said, pulling out a chair for her. "I figured you might be looking for dining companionship."

"I had thought…" her voice trailed away as she glanced back over her shoulder.

"Looking for your friend Colton? He's over there." Dan pointed to a table four or five down from theirs. "That's him with his back to us. You might get a glimpse of him if those women standing around him will move."

No wonder she hadn't seen him when she came in. Once again he was mobbed with females. She wagged her head ruefully as she sat. "He's amazing."

Dan sat across from her and lifted his shoulders in a dismissive shrug. "He doesn't do a thing for me."

She met his twinkling eyes and laughed. "I'm really glad to hear it."

Dan looked down at her tray. "Why do you punish yourself like that?" he asked, pointing to the salad.

She didn't want to confess she'd planned to sit with Colton and had hoped to fool him into believing she existed on salads. As if anybody would be dumb enough to believe she'd attained her body on lettuce and diet dressing. "I was hoping you'd have a piece of pie you'd want to share," she improvised.

He lifted a plate with a large wedge of chocolate cream pie. "Looks like today is your lucky day."

She'd forgotten what a nice smile Dan had. It wasn't movie-star perfect like Colton's, of course, but it was nice. Dan had a strong jaw and a generous mouth with straight white teeth. She liked the tiny smile lines bracketing his mouth, testimony to the good humor that seemed to radiate from him. The very best thing about his smile was the way it somehow transferred itself from his lips to his eyes when his mouth turned up in a grin.

He was an attractive man. She'd noticed right away that

he was an inch or two taller than she was, a plus in any acquaintance. He had the rangy build of an athlete—more sleek runner than bulky weight lifter. As he had on Friday, Dan wore faded blue jeans and a T-shirt that stretched over a nicely muscled chest.

This was not a man who spent hours in front of the mirror. Dan appeared to be comfortable with himself, which was probably the reason she felt so comfortable with him.

She knew instinctively that Dan was a kind man. A man who saved toppling giants and shared his dessert with hungry strangers. A man who knew how to get people to talk about themselves and possessed the rare willingness to listen to the answers.

Maddie remembered with a guilty start that she'd been so preoccupied with Colton on Friday she hadn't asked Dan anything about himself. "Tell me about Dan Willis," she said before popping a forkful of salad into her mouth.

He flashed her a self-deprecating smile. "Not much to tell."

She shook her head. "Sorry, I'm not buying that. It's payback time. I told you all about me on Friday, now it's your turn. I'll help you get started. Tell me what you do."

"I'm a photographer."

"A professional photographer?"

He nodded.

"That's interesting. What do you take pictures of?"

His laugh sounded more disgusted than amused. "At this moment, I don't know."

Uh-oh. Out-of-work photographer. No wonder he was hesitant to talk about himself. Probably pretty touchy about it. She reached across the table and patted his hand. "Don't get discouraged. Something will turn up."

He caught her hand in his, holding it up to examine it. Maddie's breath lodged midwindpipe. Wow. Amazing how his casual touch could make her insides go all squishy. She forced herself to breath. Dan's hand was warm and strong. She was amazed to see that her hand looked feminine, almost fragile when clasped in his larger one.

"This looks suspiciously like a fresh manicure to me," he teased.

She snatched her hand back in embarrassment. "It is. I had my nails done on Saturday." She didn't go on to confess that it was her first manicure ever or that it was his remark about her hands being great that had sent her racing to the nearest salon.

She'd been taught all her life to play up her assets but until she met Dan she hadn't been sure she possessed any.

Lunch ran overtime. Conversation was so easy with Dan that Maddie forgot to keep an eye on her watch.

"Oops," she said when she finally realized she'd been due back at the office ten minutes ago. "I've gotta run."

Dan smiled. "No problem. I'll look for you down here tomorrow."

Maddie's heart felt surprisingly light as she hurried toward the elevator. He didn't compare to Colton, of course, but Dan made a pretty terrific lunch date.

Chapter Four

"I'm not going with you today."

Maddie paused from loading campaign sketches into her briefcase to look at her boss. "What?"

Jack grinned. "I said I'm not going with you and Colton to Swanson Shoes today."

Maddie chuckled and resumed loading. "Very funny. You nearly gave me a heart attack. For a minute there I thought you were serious."

"I am serious. I'm not going."

She put down the briefcase to give him her full attention. "What are you talking about? Of course you're going. You're the Swanson account exec."

"Not as of ten minutes ago when I handed Colton the title."

He was serious. "Jack, why would you do that? You've been the Swanson account exec from the beginning."

"That's precisely why I'm giving the account to Colton. Think about it. We've worked so hard on this new campaign. I've pushed the creative team to the brink of a nervous breakdown with these deadlines. I would hate for all our effort to be wasted because the new president didn't want an old man directing his advertising."

"That's crazy."

Jack shook his head. "I don't think so. And neither does Colton. This morning when I voiced my concern that my presence might jeopardize our chances he admitted he'd had the same thought. We agreed that we'd be better off making a clean break from our previous association. New direction. New leadership."

"I think it stinks."

Jack smiled. "I appreciate your loyalty, but the decision stands. I'm stepping down from the account. It's up to you and Colton to salvage Swanson Shoes."

However rattled Maddie might be by the unexpected change in command, Colton appeared at the door a minute later looking his calm, cool, fabulous self. In his expensive double-breasted navy blazer and knife-creased khakis he was success personified.

"I've got the audio tapes and storyboards," he said, pointing to the large black portfolio in his right hand. "Have you got the sketches?"

Maddie scooped her briefcase off the table. "Right here."

"Excellent." Colton looked to Jack. "Unless you have any parting words of advice for us, I think we're ready."

Jack shook his head. "I have every confidence in the two of you. Make me proud."

Maddie spoke little over the ten-minute trip to Swanson Shoes. She wanted to talk, to share some witticism or pithy insight, but her tongue and brain refused to cooperate. The combination of sitting eight inches from male perfection and apprehension about the upcoming meeting with Paul Swanson left her speechless.

If Colton was nervous it didn't show. He used the drive to brief her on how they would approach the meeting. Basically he would make the pitch and she would back him up. Maddie had been relegated to a minor supporting role.

It was on the tip of her tongue to protest. After all, she was every bit as prepared to make the presentation as he was. Though she knew she had a valid argument she remained silent. Too much was riding on the outcome of this morning's meeting to entrust it to her inexperience.

Colton's confidence was contagious. By the time they reached the receptionist's desk, Maddie's misgivings about leaving Jack behind were gone.

"Good morning," Colton said to the elderly woman behind the desk. "Cue Communications here for our ten o'clock meeting with Paul Swanson."

Maddie felt a genuine compassion for the awed receptionist. At an age when she should have been immune to his beauty, it took her a full ten seconds to recover her power of speech after being broadsided by Colton's amazing smile.

"Mr. Swanson is—is expecting you," she stammered. "Second office on the left."

Maddie followed Colton into the small conference room where two men and a woman were seated around the far end of an oblong table. The man seated in the center stood and approached them, hand extended. "Hi, I'm Paul Swanson. You must be the team from Cue."

Paul Swanson wasn't what Maddie expected. She'd pictured him as a pampered little rich kid eager to flex his newfound muscle. Not so. He looked like an average guy with his feet firmly planted in reality. Far from spoiled or power crazy, he appeared earnest, no-nonsense and in no danger of being wowed by Colton's magnificence.

After the introductions were made, Maddie and Colton took their places on the opposite side of the table.

"Okay," Paul said, "show me what you've got."

Unfazed by the curt command, Colton grinned. "Ahh. A man who knows how to cut to the chase. I like that. Let's talk shoes."

For the next forty-five minutes Colton was in his element. He paced, he gestured, he varied the pitch and intensity of his voice like a seasoned evangelist. When the formal presentation was over and he opened the floor for questions, he fielded each with dazzling competency. Even the most hardened critic would have to admit he was amazing. Maddie had to sit on her hands to keep from breaking into applause.

"So, Paul," Colton said at last, "when can we implement this new campaign?"

Paul, whose noncommittal expression hadn't varied since Colton began, looked to his two colleagues then rose to his feet. "I'm sorry. It didn't grab me. I think we'll have to pass."

Maddie couldn't hear Colton's response for the roaring in her ears. They'd just lost Swanson Shoes. Her father and Jack had built Cue Communications from the rock-solid foundation of the Swanson Shoe account. The two companies had been together since the beginning. And now they were ready to call it quits.

Without being aware of moving, Maddie stood. She heard herself saying, "Not knowing the direction you wanted to take, we took the liberty of preparing another approach. Perhaps our alternate campaign will be more to your liking."

She couldn't tell who was more stunned at her pronouncement, Paul, Colton or herself. Somehow the authority in her voice must have struck a chord because both men sat and raised expectant gazes to her.

The enormity of what she'd done hit her with the force of a semi. She'd lied. Bald-faced *lied* to their oldest account. There was no secondary proposal. They'd been so confident in the MTV approach they'd concentrated their full energies on polishing it.

The room was silent. Everyone was waiting for her to say something. Maddie swallowed. Her options were simple. She could admit she'd lied, pack up their storyboards and go home in defeat, or she could punt. Somehow she thought her dad would have wanted her to punt.

To buy some time to collect her thoughts, she bent to pull the discarded notes she'd made from her research on Swanson Shoes from the bottom of her black tote bag. She smoothed the crumpled pages as best she could and stood to face Paul and his associates.

"Before I share any specifics of the campaign, let me back up a minute. In preparation for today's meeting, we researched the kind of person buying Swanson Shoes. The market has changed significantly over the years and we wanted to be certain we had our buyer clearly in our sights. Our research didn't turn up any surprises. We found that our customer is a well-educated, upwardly mobile, double-income family." Maddie rattled off a couple of the statistics she'd noted on the paper.

Though he kept his poker face in place, Maddie thought she saw Paul shift forward in his chair when she'd presented the statistics. Hmm, Paul Swanson was a numbers man.

Encouraged, she pressed on. "To best target these consumers, we propose to redirect our current focus from the price and value angle to concentrating on quality and status. To put it simply, we're going from selling Volkswagens to selling Cadillacs."

That got their attention. All three representatives from Swanson started talking at once. And none of the talk was negative.

Maddie fielded their questions as best she could and gladly relinquished the floor when Colton suggested that she might like a break and he'd be happy to review the print and media campaigns with them. Since there were no print or media campaigns to review, she was more than happy to let him bluff his way through.

Paul stopped Colton about ten minutes into what Maddie thought was a surprisingly credible spiel. "I like it," he said. "We'll want to see actual samples of the ads before we can give it our final approval, but I feel like this campaign captures the essence of Swanson Shoes. Tradition, quality and workmanship—these are the things we want to project to the market. I think Cue Communication can say it best."

The ride back to Cue was a subdued one. Like two people snatched from the cliff's edge with a surprise last-minute reprieve, neither seemed to be able to speak.

Jack met them in the hall just outside his office. Though he tried to look casual, Maddie was willing to bet he'd been pacing since they left. "Tell me how it went."

Colton gave him an abbreviated replay of the meeting with Paul Swanson. When he came to the part about Paul saying the campaign didn't grab him, Jack blanched.

Colton raised a hand to halt that train of thought. "It looked bad. I thought we were sunk until Maddie stood up and told them they might prefer plan B."

Jack looked to Maddie for confirmation. "Plan B?"

Still stunned, she could only nod.

Colton continued, "She tells Swanson about the Cadillac concept and all of a sudden the atmosphere lightens up. I believe Paul even smiled."

Colton looked at Maddie. As their eyes met they began to laugh—a hearty tension-breaking laugh that brought people from their offices to see what all the fuss was about.

Jack was still puzzled about plan B. "But you had nothing to show them—no sketches, no sample copy, no music?"

Colton shrugged. "I ad-libbed."

"Don't be so modest," Maddie said. "Jack, he was brilliant. Colton walked them step-by-step through a thirty-second television spot as though we'd written it, even humming Vivaldi for background music. He described the actors so well, I swear I could see them."

Her gaze swung back to Colton's and they laughed again at the increasingly funny memory of the averted near disaster.

Jack's secretary stepped out into the hall, pushing her way through the crowd to get to Jack. "I hate to bother you," she said, "but Burger Barn is on line one and they are furious. It seems they've run out of promotional toys three days early and their customers are up in arms."

Jack rolled his eyes and sighed. "Burger Barn goes

from one crisis to another. I guess I'd better talk them down off the roof. Maddie and Colton, I want to see you both in my office at two o'clock for a full report."

After Jack left to answer the phone, the crowd remained around Maddie and Colton. Members of the creative team began firing questions at them. "So Colton, what did you tell them the print campaign was going to look like?" "If you told them we have a television spot in mind we'd better get the specifics from you while it's still fresh in your mind."

The head copywriter looked at his watch. "It's noon now. Tell you what, we've got a meeting with the writers today. Colton, why don't you join us? You can brief us on the details."

Maddie watched Colton being led off in a flurry of congratulations and backslapping. It would have been nice to have been included in the lunch invitation. After all, it was her idea he'd embellished.

She toyed with the idea of tagging along to put in her two cents' worth but decided against it when she realized there was a bright spot to being overlooked. With Colton safely tucked away with the writers at their in-office lunch, she was free to run down to the cafeteria and splurge on a celebratory chicken-fried steak without fear of discovery.

She rode down in the elevator with Crystal the receptionist and Katie the media buyer. The two of them seemed to be in competition to come up with the most flowery adjectives for Colton. She stepped out just as the women settled on *exquisite genius*.

"Ho! What's this? Don't tell me they ran out of salads." What was it about Dan that made even the sound of his voice do funny things to her body? Like making her feel breathless and warm all over.

Maddie looked up into his smiling face then down at the half-devoured, gravy-smothered chicken-fried steak on her plate. "Nope. I splurged. I'm celebrating."

"Mind if I join you? I'm always up for a celebration."

She narrowed her eyes. "Did you bring pie?"

"Chocolate pecan."

"Excellent." She nodded toward the empty chair beside her. "Be my guest."

He chuckled as he unloaded the plates off his tray and set the empty tray on the far corner of the table. "So what are we celebrating? Did Colton manage to remember your name?"

"Even better. We saved an at-risk account."

"Oh yeah? Sounds exciting. So tell me, how does one go about saving an at-risk account?"

She told him everything. It was probably rude to bombard Dan with all the details, but he was kind enough to act interested, even asking for clarification when she glossed over a point or two.

"The whole thing was totally surreal. I still can't believe I did it," she said, finishing her story and the chicken-fried steak at the same time.

"I can. You're a smart woman. You saw a need and stepped up to fill it."

Her eyes widened to hear how much confidence he had in her abilities. "Yeah, I guess I did."

Dan slid the plate of pie between the two of them and handed her a clean fork. "So where is the other half of the brilliant team? Shouldn't Colton be here celebrating with you?"

"He's having lunch with the writers. They asked him to fill them in on the details he proposed."

Dan frowned. "I'm not complaining, but why is Colton lunching with the writers and you are sitting down here? Seems to me it was your idea that saved the day."

She shrugged. "That's not common knowledge. You see, people didn't start coming out into the hall until after my part had already been mentioned. They showed up just in time to hear the part about Colton ad-libbing a print and media campaign. They assumed the plan was his."

Dan put down his fork to glare at her. "And you didn't correct them? Colton didn't correct them?"

She looked down at the plate to avoid his eyes. "No. It didn't seem important. My boss knows. That's what matters."

"I disagree. I think the credit should go where the credit is due. And I think Colton is a jerk for stealing it."

"He didn't steal it. Besides, he was the one who came up with the ideas for the television commercials and newspaper ads. It's appropriate that he brief the writers."

Dan was not appeased. A muscle twitched in his jaw as he said, "At the very least it should have been a meeting with both members of the account team. You should be there, Maddie."

She smiled at him, partly because she wanted him to calm down and partly because she liked the fact that he'd come to her defense. He believed in her. And deep down she felt like Colton *should* have included her. "If I was there, I couldn't be here eating chocolate pecan pie with you."

"Thanks." He reached over and flicked her nose. "I'd be more appreciative of the compliment if I didn't suspect that the pie was the main attraction."

* * *

It was close to six when Maddie locked her file cabinet, hefted her tote bag on to her shoulder and clicked off her office lights. Other than the custodian pushing a vacuum, the hall was deserted. Unless they had a major project in the works, Jack closed down the office at five o'clock on Fridays. One of the perks of Cue was having a boss with a work-hard, play-hard mentality.

Maddie had heard a large group pass her office about forty-five minutes ago. They'd stopped at Colton's door to invite him to join them for drinks at one of the favorite local haunts two blocks away. She'd held her breath as she waited for them to stop by her office to repeat the invitation, but as the sound of laughing chatter faded away, she knew they weren't coming.

She shouldn't be surprised. It wasn't as though she was a regular member of the happy-hour crowd. Still… The part of her brain that stubbornly held on to faith in knights on white horses had hoped that Colton would notice she was missing from the group and insist the party wouldn't be complete without her.

For a good five minutes after they'd left she'd wrestled with the idea of going after them. She didn't require a formal invitation to show up at a bar, and if she should just happen to run into Colton and the others—what luck! She argued with herself that she was a woman of the new millennium, and as such she was master of her fate, captain of her destiny.

But in the end she stayed behind and finished up some paperwork. All the arguments in the world couldn't budge her. As a true, card-carrying romantic she wanted the thrill of being pursued.

She boarded an empty elevator. On the fourth floor it stopped its slow descent to add another passenger. The doors opened and Dan stepped on.

"Hi, Maddie," he said, flashing her a smile that sent sunshine whooshing through her veins. "Quitting time?"

She was surprised to see him in the building. Though he showed up to eat in the cafeteria regularly, she hadn't thought an out-of-work photographer needed office space. "Yeah, what about you?"

He shrugged. "I got tired of looking at the same four walls and decided to lock up and go home."

"You have an office here?"

She must not have done a very good job of masking her surprise because he sounded a bit defensive. "Yeah, I needed a place to store my cameras. I'm living in a hotel right now and until I can make more permanent arrangements I hated to leave expensive equipment lying around."

Maddie didn't know the exact figures, but she knew square footage at the Tower Building didn't come cheap. Add the expense of a hotel bill and she was certain her out-of-work friend must be waist-high in debt. Her heart did a sad little dive. Dan was a proud man. It must be hard on his wallet as well as his ego to be out of work. "If you're living in a hotel you must be overdue for a home-cooked meal. Why don't you come to my place tomorrow night and I'll feed you?"

His trademark smile widened. "Thanks. I'd like that."

Maddie rooted around in her tote bag for a pen and scrap of paper to write her address on. "Is seven good for you?" she asked, handing him the information.

"Perfect."

"See you at seven."

Chapter Five

"Madelyn, if you are there, pick up the phone. This is your mother."

Maddie resisted the temptation to let the machine take the message. No point in delaying the inevitable. She'd only have to return the call later.

"Hi, Mom."

"Hi, honey. You hadn't called in a couple of days and I was getting worried."

Maddie felt guilty. She should be glad to talk to her mother. "Sorry. We had an account presentation deadline to make and I've been so busy—"

"Speaking of busy reminds me of your sister," her mother interrupted. "Have I told you about her latest project?"

Then again, maybe Maddie *should* have let the machine answer. "No, I've been so tied up at the office—"

Her mother cut in, "She was just elected chairman of

the hospital gala for next year. Chairman is a very prestigious position, you know."

"It sounds like a major undertaking," Maddie said. "I don't see how she'll find the time—"

"All I can say is, she is amazing. I worry about her though. Juggling a busy social calendar and keeping her husband and two children happy is such a drain on her energies. Of course, she loves it."

Maddie knew her mother wasn't really worried, that she was delighted with her overachieving eldest daughter, but Maddie said what she knew her mother was expecting. "You don't need to worry about Jennifer, Mom. I'm sure she can handle it."

"You're right. She's always been so competent. And a real social butterfly." Her mother's tone of voice changed suddenly from gushing praise to cloying pity. "And what about you, Madelyn? *Anything* going on with you?"

"As a matter of fact, there is. I closed a very important deal yesterday. Saved an account. Do you remember Dad talking about Swanson Sh—"

"I didn't mean work, Madelyn," her mother chided. "I mean socially. Have you met *anybody?* You know I hate to keep bringing it up, but the family reunion is only weeks away. It'd be so nice if you brought a date this year. Why don't you take your sister up on her offer to fix you up? She said she could try to find someone. Surely with all her connections at the hospital she can come up with *somebody.*"

The tone of her mother's voice said it all. She believed the only way Maddie could get a date was through charity. Maddie tried to ignore the shaft of pain. "No. Thanks. That won't be necessary. There's a new guy at the office. I'm bringing him to the reunion."

Her mother squealed with pleasure. "Honey, why didn't you tell me?"

"It was a surprise." Major surprise. And if she thought her mother sounded surprised, imagine Colton's reaction.

"That's wonderful. What's his name?"

"Whose name?"

"The surprise date's, of course."

"Oh, him. It's Colton Hartley."

"Lovely. I can't wait to see him at the reunion."

"Me, either."

They talked for a minute or two more. After Maddie hung up, she looked at the phone in horror. She'd told her mother she had a date with Colton Hartley. What on earth had possessed her to say such a thing?

Pity. It must have been the pity in her mother's voice that had goaded Maddie into promising the undeliverable.

Over the years Maddie had grown accustomed to the well-meaning hints and advice from her mother and sister. She was proud of her ability to turn a deaf ear to them. When her father had been alive, they used to laugh off the comments together.

Now he was gone and she was left to face the digs alone. She thought she deflected them pretty well most of the time, but today's pity had cut deeply.

Because today hadn't been about grooming hints or improved posture. Today had been about who Maddie was. It hurt to think her mother thought she was a loser. Maddie knew she needed to prove her mother wrong before she began to believe it herself.

The same spirit of blind optimism that drove Maddie to declare Colton Hartley as her reunion date propelled her to the mall. The only thing better than arriving at the family reunion on Colton's gorgeous arm would be to arrive on his gorgeous arm looking fantastic.

Ordinarily she hated to shop. There was something masochistic about trying on stacks of ill-fitting clothing only to have her worst fears confirmed. She was an ugly giant.

Today she was determined to put that negative attitude behind her. She was tall, but not a giant. Hadn't Dan said so?

She smiled, wondering if Dan had any idea of the impact his words had had on her. Several times she'd caught herself repeating them like a mantra. She really owed him. She'd make something really special for tonight's dessert.

In addition to replacing attitudes, she'd decided to upgrade her image as well. No more would she dress herself in safe, dreary black, trying in vain to minimize her size and blend in. No more would she devote her energies to drawing attention away from herself. Today she would find something bright and colorful. Something with confidence written all over it. Something that would elicit praise, not pity.

Like a general poised for battle and committed to his life or death mission, Maddie marched across the gleaming marble floors of the department store to women's sportswear. She came to a screeching halt at the edge of the department. Old habits died hard. Seeing the racks of clothing brought back a flood of memories of past failures and insecurities. Of shopping trips with her perfect sister that invariably drew unflattering comparisons.

Maddie took a deep breath, trying to bolster her flagging resolve. I am tall, she repeated to herself, not a giant. And I have great hands.

She threw her shoulders back and stepped up to the first rounder crowded with cropped pants and matching tops. Hmmm. That might be a cute look. Stylish but casual. She pushed past hanger after hanger of soft pastels. Though the colors were mouth-watering and the fabric lovely, she knew from past disasters that the delicate shades were anathema to her own coloring.

The petal pink her fair mother and sister wore so successfully made Maddie look peaked. The buttercup yellows and greens they favored made Maddie look as if she were terminally ill with a liver disorder.

She pressed on. From pastels she gravitated to the neon brights of a neighboring rounder. No way. In the orange shirt and matching shorts she'd look like a six-foot emergency flare. Or a bigger-than-life Popsicle.

As she bypassed the whites as too impractical and the blacks as too predictable she realized she'd come to the far edge of the department without finding a thing.

Maddie was close to despair when an elevated rack sitting off by itself caught her eye. Sundresses. Darling little wisps of summery fabric with spaghetti straps and fluttery hems.

She moved closer to consider this new option. A sundress would be perfect. A sundress said cool, feminine, flirty. All the things she wanted others to see in her.

Maddie picked up the first one, a royal blue and white print. Simple. Sexy. Divine. As she pressed it to her heart she could almost see herself at Colton's side, confidence radiating from her.

Her relatives would be flabbergasted at her transformation from self-conscious moth to dazzling butterfly. Best of all, for once she'd have Colton's full attention. He wouldn't be able to take his eyes off her…

"May I help you?"

Maddie wrenched her thoughts from the clouds to focus on the diminutive sales clerk, an elderly woman with bright red lips and a beaded chain dangling from the temples of her cat's-eye glasses.

"May I help you, dear?"

"Yes." Maddie lifted the sundress. "I'm looking for something to wear to a reunion. A sundress."

The saleslady looked from Maddie to the dress and back to Maddie. "Is it a gift?"

"No. It's for me."

The clerk snatched the dream from Maddie's fingers and rehung it with a clank. "I don't think a size two will do you much good," she said with a chuckle.

Her experienced fingers sifted through the fabric confections, stopping to pull a much larger version of the same dress from the rack.

"This one looks like it'll go around you, though I'm guessing it'll be too short. What are you," she asked, not unkindly, "Six feet?"

"Five eleven," Maddie corrected automatically. She took the replacement from the sales clerk. Was it her imagination or did the blue and white print that looked so chic in a size two take on the appearance of a wide expanse of bad bathroom wallpaper in the larger size?

"Do you want to try it on? The dressing rooms are over there."

Maddie held the dress against herself for a fraction of a second then handed it back to the clerk. "No, I don't think so. You're right. It's too short."

The woman hung it up and continued on through the remainder of the dresses, finally shaking her head. "I'm sorry, dear. I don't have anything that will work for you. But I did just get a new shipment of calf-length dresses. I think I saw one in black that might work for you."

Maddie swallowed a discouraged sigh. Always black. Maybe it was a sign. If it was, she hated to think what it might mean. "No, thanks. I don't think I'm in the mood to try anything on today."

She gave herself a pep talk on the way home. Her lack of success at the mall was really a blessing in disguise she told her reflection in the rearview mirror. She'd been too hasty racing out to the mall for a new look; it was a dumb idea, obviously a knee-jerk reaction to her mother's pity.

The fact was, she had a lot of nice things hanging in her closet that she could wear to the reunion. And there was nothing wrong with the color black. Black was classic. And slimming.

Chapter Six

Dan transferred the tissue-wrapped bouquet from his right hand to his left and rang the doorbell.

Maddie appeared at the door almost immediately. "Hi Dan. Right on time."

He liked the way her eyes telegraphed her pleasure at seeing him. When her mouth turned up in a wide smile his focus automatically shifted to her lips. She'd brushed on a hint of gloss that emphasized the fullness of her lower lip. Absently, he licked his own lips, wondering if the gloss was flavored.

He blinked to clear his mind and coughed to clear his suddenly clogged throat. "Actually, I was early. I've been sitting in the lobby for the last thirty minutes reading a three-day-old newspaper someone left behind."

"You should have come on up."

He shook his head. "Seems like my momma once told

me it was bad manners to show up too early. Something about not rushing a lady."

"That was thoughtful of you, but unnecessary. Friends don't need to stand on ceremony." She stepped aside. "Come on in."

He propped the camera bag he'd carried in against the wall and waited until she closed the door to hand her the bouquet.

"Flowers for me?" She sounded as though he'd presented her with a rare treat. He regretted that he hadn't had his camera ready to capture the expression of surprised delight on her face as she buried her nose in the bouquet. "They're beautiful."

"Beautiful flowers for a beautiful lady." Dan's mouth snapped shut. Where did that come from? he wondered. Trite phrases and sweet talk were not his style. But when he saw her head bent over the blooms, the words had just slipped out. And they weren't empty flattery. They were the gospel truth.

Maddie dismissed the compliment with a disbelieving laugh. "That's sweet of you to say. You must be blind as well as thoughtful. Come on into the kitchen while I put these in water."

He noted the term *beauty* did not extend to her clothing. She was wearing a long tunic thing over flowy pants— like something off the cover of the Beatles' *Abbey Road* album, though in black. Dan followed her flapping hem down the hall to the kitchen.

"Mmm. Smells great in here," he said with an appreciative sniff.

"I hope you like lasagna," she said over her shoulder as she filled a clear glass vase with water.

"Love it."

She placed the flowers in the vase and handed it to him. "Do me a favor? Find a place for these while I fix us something to drink?"

He crossed the hall into the living room and his jaw dropped. The room was a showplace.

He'd known from the moment he walked in the front door that the architecture of the apartment was excellent. The proportions of the rooms were good and the high ceilings and wide molding said first class. What amazed him was what Maddie had done with the space.

Elegant cream-colored sofas and pretty polished mahogany tables were arranged in a cozy grouping on a thick oriental rug. The walls and drapes were also a creamy yellow-white giving the room the kind of understated elegance found in magazines. Plump throw pillows in rich jewel-toned silks were scattered in artful clumps to keep the pristine décor from being bland, and a lipstick-pink damask chaise lounge by the window introduced just the right note of whimsy. And sensuality.

"Wow."

Maddie appeared beside him, a glass of iced tea in each hand. "Wow what?"

He swept a hand around the room. "This place. It's fabulous."

"Thank you."

"I mean it. It's really great. Did you have a decorator?"

"Nope. I did it myself."

"You're kidding."

"I think I'll try to ignore the shock I hear in your voice and take that as a compliment."

He *was* shocked. In his experience a person's home reflected the owner. Frankly, he'd expected something different. Something shapeless and black.

She placed her two glasses on an end table and slid the vase from his unresisting fingers. She carried it to the coffee table and placed it in the center, turning the vase until she had it just so. She stepped back to study the effect. "They are lovely. Thank you."

"No problem. I owed you for the invitation to dinner."

She grinned. "You better save your thanks until you taste it. I just took the lasagna out and put in the garlic bread. It's got about fifteen more minutes to bake. Would you like a tour while you wait?"

He was glad she volunteered so he didn't have to ask. Now that he'd seen the living room he wouldn't rest until he discovered whether the remainder of the place lived up to that first impression.

It did. The rest of the apartment confirmed it. Maddie had a killer sense of style. Her use of rich colors and elegant furnishings told a much different story than her personal appearance. The apartment was sensuous, her clothing sexless. The apartment screamed good taste, her look shouted no taste at all. It didn't make sense.

Dan picked up a framed eight-by-ten photograph from an antique table in the hall. "Is this your family?"

She smiled. "Yes. That was taken a few years ago, before my dad died. He and my mom and my sister Jennifer had come down to school to visit."

Dan studied the picture. Maddie hadn't changed much since then. Her hair in the picture was long but rather than being propped on top of her head it was pulled back in a severe, eye-stretching ponytail.

She stood between her father and her sister, her proud

father's arm resting on her shoulders. She and her dad wore mirror-image grins for the camera.

There was a marked contrast between one half of the family and the other. Maddie and her father were tall and dark while her mother and sister were petite and fair.

"There's no denying the family resemblance between you and your father," Dan said.

Maddie smiled. "Everybody says that. My mother used to call us the twin peaks."

Though he heard no bitterness, Dan suspected being referred to as a mountain had something to do with Maddie's low self-esteem. "Your mother and sister could pass for twins."

"Isn't that sickening," Maddie agreed without malice. "Imagine the laughs I get when I tell people that the five-foot-three-inch, size-two beauty is my big sister."

Ouch. One more reason to see herself as a giant.

He returned the photograph to the table. "As an only child I always thought it would be great to have a sibling. Are you and your sister close?"

Maddie nodded. "As close as two people going in completely different directions can be. Much to my mother's delight, Jennifer got married right out of college to a plastic surgeon in Dallas. Between raising two kids and doing all the social things that a doctor's wife does she barely has time to sit down and catch her breath. Because of her social schedule and my work we don't see each other often. But she's really sweet. Other than being beautiful and a chronic overachiever, she's the perfect sister."

A buzzer rang in the kitchen. "Time to eat."

Maddie served dinner in the formal dining room. They

feasted on crisp green salad, buttery garlic bread and the thickest, cheesiest lasagna Dan had ever sunk his teeth into.

"That was delicious, Maddie," Dan said placing his fork on the table at last. "We'll have to add amazing cook on top of the list of all your other accomplishments. I'd like to have seconds but I think I'll explode."

"Then I guess I'll have to throw away the lemon chiffon pie I made for dessert."

His face lit up. "Are you kidding? Lemon chiffon pie? Does it have whipped cream on top?"

She nodded. "About an inch and a half thick."

"Aw man, that's one of my favorites." He patted his stomach. "Tell you what. Give me an hour to digest and I'll be primed for pie."

Maddie poured them each a cup of coffee and led him out to the balcony off the living room. It was a narrow strip of concrete, ringed with a lacy black wrought-iron railing. Besides the half dozen clay pots of colorful flowers there was a small gas grill pushed to the far corner and a round glass-topped bistro table with two chairs to the right of the door.

The sun had started its descent, taking the oppressive heat with it. Muffled sounds of traffic drifted upwards on snatches of cool breeze.

"This is great." Dan pulled out Maddie's chair for her. "The view is terrific from up here." He bent to retrieve his camera from the bag he'd carried out.

Maddie slanted him a suspicious glance. "What's that?"

"It's a camera."

"I can see that, smart guy. Why do you have a camera?"

"To take pictures."

She narrowed her eyes at his deliberate obtuseness. "Of what?"

"You. I thought it might be fun to take a few shots." His casual answer didn't begin to explain his near obsession to photograph her. The idea had taken root the very first time he'd met her. He wondered if he could capture on film the vulnerability and freshness, the inner beauty that radiated from her. With each meeting the need intensified. Maddie was a challenge he couldn't wait to face.

"Oh, no," she said, waving her hands in front of her face as if to ward off blows. "I hate to have my picture taken. Trust me, you don't want to photograph me. I'm terminally unphotogenic."

He cocked a brow. "Can it be that Maddie Sinclair is camera shy? That the woman who took on Swanson Shoes is afraid to have her picture taken?"

She bristled up. "I'm not afraid. I'm ugly."

When he opened his mouth to protest she interrupted. "Don't look so unhappy. I'm doing you a favor. Probably saving your camera from irreparable damage."

"You're not ugly, just chicken." He scooped the camera bag off the floor and unzipped the lid. "That's okay. I won't force the issue. I only wanted to get a little practice."

"Practice?" Maddie reached over to stop him from placing the camera in the bag.

He stilled his hand. "Yeah. It's important to keep my skills sharp even though I'm between jobs."

He could see the second when she gave up the battle. Her expression softened and her shoulders relaxed. "Okay," she said, "You can take a few pictures if it's only for practice. But don't show them to anybody, okay?"

His heart broke at the vulnerability in her voice. "Okay."

She sat up broomstick straight and lifted her hand to her

hair, checking for strays. She drew a deep breath and said, "I'm ready."

Her face looked stiff. Her smile cold. No way he'd settle for a shot like that. "You don't need to pose. If it's okay with you I'll just fool around with the camera while we talk. If I end up with a few pictures, fine, if not, fine."

She looked uncertain. "Okay."

It took a while to restore the easy camaraderie they'd shared over dinner. For at least five minutes she stared distrustfully at his camera and only answered direct questions with monosyllables.

To put her at ease Dan raised the camera to his eye and looked away from her, shooting random photographs of pedestrians down below or buildings across the street.

Eventually they were laughing and talking again and he was able to sneak a couple of candid shots. "I have an idea," he said as he popped out a spent roll of film and fitted a new roll into the camera. "Would you be willing to take your hair down for a couple of pictures? I'd like to experiment with a different look. For practice."

"Is it necessary?"

He nodded, his heart racing as he awaited her answer. He might as well admit he was indulging a fantasy that had been flashing through his mind all evening: the repressed beauty lets down her hair and is suddenly transformed into an alluring siren.

"If you think it will help…" Obviously reluctant, Maddie reached up to pull the pins from her hair.

"Let me." Dan put down his camera and moved behind Maddie. One by one he gently pulled the long brown pins from her hair.

As a photographer it was not unusual for him to adjust

a model's hair or clothing to get the shot he wanted, but until tonight he'd never recognized the intimacy of what he was doing. Her neck was warm and smooth where his fingers brushed against it. As each lock of loosed hair tumbled down her back it released a soft flowery fragrance. When the last pin was removed he was tempted to grab a handful of the fragrant silk and bury his face in it.

"Okay, now," he instructed, "shake it out."

The movement didn't have the effect he expected. Instead of falling in silken waves down her back her naturally curly hair sprang to life. It didn't drift down her back in velvety coils. It shot off her scalp in wiry abandon. The hair seemed to grow right before his eyes.

"Wow."

"It's a mess, isn't it? Like kudzu. You can see why I have to keep it pinned up. I'm half afraid if I left it down it would take on a life of its own and smother me." She laughed, but he could hear the insecurity in the sound.

He'd never seen so much hair in his life. It was not only long, past the middle of her back, but thick. If he had to describe it in one word it would be *overwhelming*.

"It's not a mess," he said as he picked up his camera and moved across the table from her. "It's amazing."

This time he didn't try to distract her by photographing anything but her. He shot up another roll of film as he played with different angles and lighting.

When the camera whirred, signaling the end of another roll, Maddie said, "Enough practice. Time for dessert."

"Sounds like a deal."

Once again seated in the dining room Dan forked the first bite of pie into his mouth. "Mmm. This is incredible."

"Thank you."

He looked at her. "You cook like an angel. You decorate like a pro. You are full of surprises."

"So I've heard," she said with a laugh.

"Huh?"

"My mother said the very same thing to me just this morning when I told her I was bringing Colton Hartley to my family reunion."

"That *is* a surprise."

"Actually, it's a lie." She went back to eating her pie.

Dan placed his fork on his plate and looked at her expectantly. "Aw, come on now. You can't leave me hanging."

Maddie swallowed her bite. "It's a long story."

"No problem. I've got time and we've still got three-quarters of a pie. I'm not going anywhere."

She sighed. "My family has a reunion every year—my mother's side of the family."

"Sounds fun."

She shook her head. "Not."

He resumed eating. "I've gotta tell you, I'm having a hard time picturing any gathering that features potato salad and watermelon being a bad thing."

"It's not a bad thing. It's awkward." She gave a mirthless laugh. "Actually, I'm awkward. In our family, a reunion is a time to catch up on what everyone has been doing over the past year. A time to introduce boyfriends, gossip about spouses and brag about kids. I don't have any of those things.

"And that's okay," she hurried on, "because I have work. But the relatives don't see it that way. They look at me and wag their heads as if to say, 'Poor Maddie.' I don't usually let it bother me but when my mom called me this morning and practically called me a loser, I lost it. Before I could think, I opened my big mouth and out popped a date with Colton."

"I don't know why you want a date with that credit-stealing, self-absorbed jerk anyway."

Maddie looked him straight in the eye. "Because he's perfect. And if I could get a date with him I would prove to my family that I am not a loser."

There was so much Dan wanted to say, reassurances he wanted to give. But it wouldn't do any good. He could see how deeply she believed those words. "Can't you just show up at the reunion without him? Say that he had some last-minute medical emergency?"

She shook her head. "No, they'd see right through that. Then I'd really look pitiful."

"So what are you going to do?"

Determination shone in her eyes. "I'm going to ask Colton to the reunion. It won't be so hard. Our relationship has already progressed in the short time I've know him."

That was news to Dan. "How so?"

She grinned. "He remembers my name."

Dan laughed. "Wow, at the rate things are going you two will be married by Christmas."

"Be sure to keep the date open."

Maddie walked Dan to the door with an aluminum pan of lasagna and half the pie to take home. "Can you carry all this?" she asked, transferring the leftovers to him.

He slid the strap of his camera bag over his shoulder and took the pans. "I've got it. Thanks for everything. I had a great time."

"Me, too." She opened the door to let him out. "We'll have to do it again soon."

"Deal." Dan started through the door then paused. "I know you're planning to take Colton to the reunion, but if things should fall through, I'd be happy to pinch-hit. I'm a big fan of reunions."

She smiled. "Thanks. I'll remember that."

It was the smile that did it.

Dan hadn't planned to kiss her. For Pete's sake, she'd just finished outlining her plans to snag the great Colton. But then she smiled. A smile of affection and gratitude. A smile so open, so beautiful that he couldn't resist.

He leaned in, shifting the pans in his arms so he could get close, and brushed his lips across hers. Her mouth was soft, her lips slightly parted in surprise. Though he ached to deepen the kiss, to taste the mouth he'd obsessed about, he pulled back. "Goodnight, then."

"Goodnight."

Chapter Seven

The Monday meeting was running long. Maddie was having trouble focusing on business because the account status reports weren't nearly as interesting as the memory of Dan's surprise kiss last night.

As the account executive droned on about forecasted sales, Maddie closed her eyes, trying to recreate the moment. It had happened so quickly. One minute they had been talking and the next minute Dan had been leaning toward her. Maddie marveled at how natural it had been to meet him halfway; how right it had felt to close her eyes and tip her mouth to his.

She ran her tongue experimentally over her lips, trying to remember the kiss. Sweet. He'd tasted sweet. And firm. His mouth had been warm and firm. Mmm.

Maddie's eyes flew open as the hum rumbled in the back of her throat. What was she doing? She didn't have time to be fantasizing over a kiss. She had more pressing matters to consider, specifically, how in the world she was going to land a date with Colton. She became so engrossed in her plot to capture his affection that she didn't hear her name being called.

"Earth to Maddie," Jack said, getting a laugh from the assembled staff. "Would you mind joining Colton and me up here for a moment?"

Her face flamed red as she clutched her yellow pad to her chest and, with shoulders hunched, crossed the now-silent room to join Jack and Colton standing at the head of the table.

Jack stood between them and hooked an arm around their shoulders. "For any of you who managed to miss the news on Friday, Maddie and Colton saved the Swanson Shoes account."

The room erupted into polite applause.

"After our planned campaign failed to grab the new CEO's interest, they pulled an eleventh-hour pitch out of thin air and got Paul's signature on the dotted line."

More applause punctuated by the occasional whoop or whistle.

"In order to best serve our client, we are restructuring the account team. I have stepped down as the managing account executive of Swanson Shoes and have named Colton as my replacement."

The applause was frenzied, the kind that would accompany the announcement of a cure for cancer.

"In addition, I'm promoting Maddie to account executive to round out the Swanson Shoes team."

More applause, and this time it was for her.

It didn't get any better than this. Maddie's heart could

have burst with sheer joy. At the end of the meeting, the staff stood in line to shake her hand and congratulate her on her promotion. As a sign of solidarity, Colton stood by her side in the impromptu receiving line to accept his congratulations.

When the conference room was empty except for Jack, Colton and herself, Maddie said to Jack, "Thank you."

"For what?"

"For giving me the promotion."

"I didn't *give* you anything," he said. "You earned it."

Colton said, "Give yourself some credit, Maddie. The tenacity you showed with Paul Swanson had account executive written all over it. You're bright, articulate and think fast on your feet. I completely misread the Swanson Shoes' account. If it had been solely up to me on Friday, I'd have lost the business."

Maddie floated in a dreamlike trance out of the conference room and down the hall. A promotion! Wait till Dan heard about this. He'd be so proud of her he'd flip.

More amazing than her promotion were the compliments from Colton. He'd noticed she was bright and articulate. Dan would be happy to know that Colton was giving her the credit she was due.

Maddie thought about the expression on Colton's face when he'd praised her at the meeting. He'd actually looked her in the eyes as he spoke. Compliments *and* eye contact—could a date be far behind?

Maddie ducked into the ladies' room on the way back to her office. As she closed the door to her stall she heard someone enter the room.

"Man, that was a long meeting." Maddie recognized the voice as Crystal's.

"Yeah, I had six messages waiting for me on my voice mail." That had to be Katie the media buyer.

Maddie could hear the rattling sounds of them rooting in their purses. Probably primping before they went back to their desks.

After a moment or two Crystal said, "It sure is good news about Swanson Shoes."

"No kidding. I heard Jack's secretary say he was in a panic. He really thought we were going to lose it."

"I'm excited about Maddie getting promoted."

"She was definitely due," Katie said. "She works hard." Maddie smiled.

"Can you imagine getting to work on a team with Colton?"

"No, but if I'm ever asked you can be sure I'm going to request lots of overtime."

"I envy Maddie. She's one lucky woman."

"Get real. She works with him, same as we do. It's not like they're a couple or anything."

"Wouldn't that be weird? Like Beauty and the Beast."

Maddie winced. She didn't have any trouble figuring out who was the Beauty and who was the Beast. She waited to step out of the stall until the giggling faded away and the sound of the door swinging shut signaled that the women had left.

She tilted her head side to side and studied her reflection as she washed her hands. She knew she wasn't much to look at, but a beast?

She dried her hands on a paper towel and walked back to her office, head held high. She wouldn't let a catty remark get her down. Sticks and stones and all that. Besides, if she remembered her fairy tales correctly, Beauty and the Beast lived happily ever after.

At noon she closed down the file she was working on and pulled her purse out of the cabinet. Time to put her plans into operation. Since she and Colton were officially a team there was no reason for her to feel shy about asking him to lunch.

She rapped twice on his half-opened door and stepped in. He was working on his computer.

"Hi. Interested in grabbing some lunch?" She was proud of the casual way that came out, as if she asked out fabulous men all the time.

He glanced up. "Sorry. I've made plans with friends."

She didn't allow her cheerful expression to fade. "No problem. Maybe another time."

"Yeah."

Maddie stepped onto the elevator and rode it to the lobby. She didn't think a woman who'd just received a promotion should eat alone. She needed to be with someone who could enjoy her good fortune with her. She needed a friend. She needed Dan.

She searched the cafeteria for him before stepping into the serving line. He wasn't seated at any of the center tables. The room wasn't as crowded as usual so she had a clear view of the occupants. Dan wasn't there.

Her previously ebullient spirits fell flat. Funny how much she'd been looking forward to seeing him, to feeling that rush of warmth he never failed to produce. She had even planned to suggest they splurge on two pieces of pie in honor of the occasion.

She chastised herself for not having his phone number. Halfway to the tray pickup she remembered that he'd said he had an office on the fourth floor. She wasn't really hungry. She'd just pop upstairs and tell him her good news. She stepped out of line and hurried to the elevators.

Unlike the thirty-second floor of the Tower Building that was dedicated solely to Cue Communications, the fourth floor housed many smaller businesses; each one was identified by a discreet plaque mounted to the right of the office door.

Maddie moved slowly down the hall, stopping at each door to read the name of the tenant. Dan's plaque read simply Dan Willis.

She thought she might drop him the marketing tip that he should add the word *photographer* beside his name. Being out of work, he could use all the advertising he could get. He might be able to pick up a little business from the walk-by traffic in the hall.

She stepped inside his office. Country music blared from a radio on the desk.

"Hello?" she called, pitching her voice to be heard above Alan Jackson. "Anybody home?"

No answer.

She walked a little farther into the room and tried again, "Dan, are you here?"

A muffled 'just a minute' filtered through one of the three interior doors.

"Okay." She looked around the sparsely decorated space for a place to sit. Since the only furniture in the room was a desk and a chair her choices were limited.

Bless his heart. He was obviously operating on a very limited budget. He probably couldn't afford anything else. Still, appearances were important in business. He'd need to spruce the place up if he wanted to attract paying customers. It didn't affect the quality of his work, but people made judgments based on outward appearance.

She settled back into the chair, a comfortable high-backed black leather one that she suspected he'd blown his entire setup budget on, and drummed her fingers on the metal desk he must have salvaged from a Dumpster.

She mentally redecorated the office while she waited. First thing he needed was additional seating. The room wasn't that large; a loveseat would do for a start. She had a nice one in one of the bedrooms in her apartment, upholstered in a handsome stripe. She wondered if he'd be offended if she offered it to him. If he took it well she'd throw in a nice low table to place in front of the loveseat.

Her gaze traveled to the walls. At least he'd had the good sense to hang photographs. From her vantage point behind the desk she admired the dramatic effect of two rows of eleven-by-fourteen pictures, about twenty in all, framed in plain black frames.

Minutes ticked by. Garth Brooks was singing the cute little love song that had since been made into a cola commercial. Dan hadn't made an appearance yet. Restless, Maddie walked over to the first of the framed photographs to get an idea of the quality of Dan's work.

It wasn't until she moved closer that she realized the pictures weren't photographs at all, but enlarged magazine covers. She frowned. The man had no marketing sense at all. He wasn't likely to attract customers with other people's work. He must have really admired the photographers who had worked with the models and superstars because he'd gone to the trouble of getting them autographed.

She leaned in toward the closest cover, a gorgeous supermodel posed on the front, to read the scrawled note: Dan, as always, it's been great working with you. Cindy.

Maddie's head snapped back. To Dan from Cindy?

The next cover, another woman's magazine with a well-known model on the front, carried a similar inscription. As did the next. And the next.

"Hi, Maddie, I thought that sounded like you. Sorry I kept you waiting. I was developing those pictures I took of you the other night."

Maddie whirled to face him. "You! You're Dan Willis."

He looked puzzled. "Yeah. So?"

She pointed a trembling hand toward the covers. "You're Dan Willis. *The* Dan Willis."

Stunned, he said, "You've heard of me?"

"Well, no, but I recognize your work. This *is* your work, isn't it?"

"Yeah."

She covered her face with her hands. "Omigosh."

"What?"

She peeked at him through her fingers. "I can't believe I let you take pictures of me the other night. I'm so embarrassed."

"Why would you be embarrassed?" He took a step toward her. "They're great. I can't wait for you to see them."

Maddie retreated a step. "I know you are too kind a person to make fun of me, so I can only suppose that you are deranged or something. Is that why you're not working right now? You've had some sort of breakdown?"

He stopped and frowned. "No, I didn't have a breakdown. I was just burned out."

"Burnout, breakdown—same thing. That is the only rational explanation for why you'd want to photograph me—the Beast."

"Beast?" He grimaced. "Where do you come up with this kind of stuff?"

"I didn't come up with it." She tried to still her quivering lower lip. "The girls at the office did."

"Aw, Maddie." Dan closed in to gather her into his arms. "Honey, you shouldn't listen to stuff like that."

"I tried not to," she sobbed into the shoulder of his black T-shirt. "I told myself it didn't matter. I mean, there's more to a person than looks. It's the inside that matters, right?"

She pulled back from his arms, brushing the tears off her cheeks with the back of her hand. "I don't know why I'm asking you that. For heaven's sake, you make your living working with people who have made fortunes with their looks."

"If I've learned anything behind the camera it's that the most perfect packages are the emptiest. There are exceptions of course," he tipped up his shoulder to indicate the models on his wall, "but for the most part they have nothing else—no personality, no compassion. For many of them, their only asset is their looks."

Maddie sniffled. "That doesn't sound so bad to me."

He chuckled as he cradled her face in his hands. "Maddie, there is something about you, a depth to you that I've never seen anywhere else. You have more beauty than all those models put together. That's why I wanted to photograph you. To try to capture that inner beauty."

"Ugly people get depth and inner beauty. Doesn't seem fair."

"You're not ugly."

Maddie rolled her eyes.

"I'm shooting straight with you. You are entirely too hard on yourself. It's time to make peace with who you are, Maddie. Play up your assets. When was the last time you did something for yourself? When was the last time you treated yourself to a makeover or a new do?"

She reached a hand to her hair. "I get trims every six months."

"Very sensible, but it doesn't count as a treat."

"The best treat for my hair would be to cut it all off. I think about doing it all the time, but my dad loved long hair."

"You don't think he liked it so much that he'd sentence you to a lifetime of misery just to please him, do you?"

"I don't know," she said with a shrug.

"I'm not going to lecture you on style. You've got plenty of your own. Furthermore," he said, stepping closer to catch her face in his hands once again, "I like you just the way you are."

There it was again. That infusion of heat, like a shaft of sunlight. She sighed. "Thanks. Hey, I almost forgot why I came up here. I got a promotion. I'm an official account executive on the Swanson Shoes' account."

"Congratulations. You deserve it. It's good to know your boss recognizes talent."

"Colton, too. Do you know he told me that I'm bright and articulate and think fast on my feet? He admitted in front of Jack that he'd misread the situation with Swanson Shoes and said that he'd have lost the account without me."

Dan's hands dropped from her face and his dark brows shot up in disbelief. "Humility and insight from Colton? That's surprising."

"You were completely wrong about him, Dan. He didn't take the credit for my work. He even said that I have account executive written all over me."

"Does that mean he can read?"

"Don't be snide. He's not one of those pretty, empty packages you were talking about. He may be too gorgeous for his own good, and maybe a little overconfident, but deep down I think he's a very nice guy."

"Very deep down," Dan muttered.

"Be nice," Maddie scolded. "We're talking about my new partner. Do you know what this means?"

"He'll be asking you to carry his mirror in that big purse of yours?"

"Very funny. It means that he and I will be working closely together. A lot."

"Oh goody."

Maddie huffed in exasperation. "Dan, I don't think you appreciate the situation. Two people thrown together with a common goal? This is the perfect setup for an office romance. I'll have my date to the reunion in no time. Time!" She glanced at her watch. "Heavens! I was due back at the office ten minutes ago. I had planned to take you to lunch at the cafeteria to celebrate my big promotion. I guess it'll have to wait."

As she dashed to the door she said, "Set aside some time on Saturday and we'll celebrate."

"It's a date."

After she left, Dan picked up the phone and dialed long distance. "Let me speak to Thomas, please. Yeah, I know he's busy. Tell him it's Dan Willis."

Chapter Eight

Colton appeared at Maddie's door at four-thirty Friday afternoon. "Hey Maddie, you got a minute?"

For you, she thought, a lifetime. "Sure, what do you need?"

"Jack just brought me some stuff on the new Electronics Era account. He asked if we would take a look at it."

"Be glad to." She glanced around her small office. "I'd ask you to pull up a chair, but I don't have one."

"No problem." He ducked out, reappearing moments later with a chair he'd filched from the reception area. He hefted it over her desk to position it beside hers.

"This is cozy." He climbed around her trash basket to squeeze in beside her.

"Very," Maddie squeaked. She cleared her throat. "So tell me, what's up with Electronics Era?"

Smooth, she thought, mentally patting herself on the

back. After the one unfortunate squeak, she'd managed to school her voice to cool professional interest. She was certain he couldn't tell her heart was pounding its way out of her chest.

"Jack says they're ready for a change. I guess they figured that rapidly firing brand names of stereo equipment onto the screen isn't getting the job done."

Maddie nodded. "Their ads are always so schlocky."

Colton flashed her a mind-erasing grin. "Jack wants us to toss some replacement ideas around. I got the impression that if he likes what we come up with, he may give us the account. I told him we'd get back with him on Monday."

The impossible deadline got her attention. "Wow, that's fast."

"Yeah, but I've got you on my team. With your insight and talent this will be a piece of cake."

Her ego inflated along with her heart rate. "It might take some work over the weekend," she suggested hopefully.

"Yeah, I thought of that. Are you doing anything?"

Omigosh. It had already begun. Of course, it was only a working date, but it was a good start on an office romance. "No, I'm completely free."

"I was hoping you'd say that. I'm booked solid through Sunday, but since your calendar is open maybe you can flesh out any ideas we come up with this afternoon."

"Oh."

"I know it's shabby to dump it all on you. I'd never have made other plans if I'd known Jack had something for us to do."

"That's okay. I understand."

"You are so great, Maddie. I feel like I really lucked out to have you on my team."

That was the opening she'd been waiting for. He thought she was great and that he was lucky to be working with her. Okay, it wasn't a declaration of love or even an invitation to a working date, but she was desperate. The reunion was only weeks away and she'd promised to produce him as her escort.

Maddie cleared her throat. "Speaking of teams, my family is getting together in a few weeks for a reunion—you know, barbeque, sack races, horseshoes. The competition is always stiff so I'm looking for recruits. What are you doing on Saturday, three weeks from tomorrow?"

Colton frowned. "Reunion, huh? Sounds great. It really does. But I don't think I can make it. Saturdays aren't good for me." He patted her on the back. "Thanks for the invite, though."

"Maddie? What are you doing hanging around here so late on a Friday night? I want you—" Jack walked far enough into the doorway to see Dan leaning against the file cabinet. "Oh hello, I didn't realize Maddie had company."

"Come on in, Jack," Maddie said. "I want you to meet my friend."

Dan straightened and extended his hand. "Dan Willis."

"I'm Jack Benson. It's a pleasure to meet you, Dan. You must be the photographer Maddie told me about. She said you might be looking for some work."

Maddie and Dan exchanged glances. "Well, uh—"

"I'm always interested in new talent. We're currently planning a shoot of patio furniture. A nice two-page layout in the *Star Telegram*. Have you got a portfolio of your work? If so I'd love for you to bring it by." Jack pulled a business card from his shirt pocket and handed it to Dan. "Call my secretary and set up an appointment."

"Thank you."

Jack turned his attention back to Maddie. "I hope you're not planning to make a late night of it."

"I've got a couple more things to do before I call it quits."

"Do you want me to run down to the cafeteria and pick up something for you to eat before I go?"

"No thanks. Dan and I just ordered a pizza."

"Oh." Jack directed a pointed stare at Dan while he spoke to Maddie. "The housekeeping staff will be here so you won't be alone. And when you're ready to go be sure to have Dan walk you to your car. Things are pretty deserted in the parking garage after hours on weekends. I'd feel better knowing you had an escort."

"I'll take care of her, sir."

Jack's expression softened. "Good. You two have fun. Goodnight."

Maddie waited until the sound of Jack's footfalls faded away. "That was awkward. Sorry."

"Because of the job offer? Don't be. I detect the hand of my friend trying to rustle up some work for her unemployed cafeteria buddy. I'm flattered you were worried about me."

"*Was* worried. Past tense. Remember, I saw all those autographed covers on the wall. Now I have no qualms whatsoever about letting you pay for the pizza. I will, however, spring for the tip for the driver. Actually, I was apologizing for the father-entrusting-his-treasured-daughter-to-the-unworthy-suitor routine."

Dan grinned. "Are you kidding? I liked it. I felt like I was sixteen again."

"It's so rare that I'm with a man, he probably thought he'd better seize the opportunity to play overprotective father. With my dating history, he may not have another chance."

"That just goes to show how stupid my gender can be." Dan lounged against the file cabinet, his arms folded across his chest. "Speaking of stupid, where's Colton?"

She frowned up at him. "He's not stupid. And to answer your question, the posse showed up for him about five-thirty. I think they were going clubbing."

"Isn't that special? Maddie works while Colton plays. Or am I wrong in assuming that you are working on something that the two of you should be doing together?"

"You're wrong. Well, not exactly wrong," Maddie amended, carefully avoiding his gaze. "I'm finishing up a proposal he and I started this afternoon."

Dan pushed away from the file cabinet to stand in front of her desk. "This is the weekend. If he can play, you can too. Let's go to a movie. You can finish it up on Monday."

She frowned. "I would, but it's important I do it now. Colton promised Jack we'd have it ready to show him on Monday."

"I see. It's important enough for you to spend your weekend working, but not important enough for Mr. Hotshot to change his plans."

"You're not being fair. He felt really badly about leaving it all to me. But it was so last-minute, he couldn't get out of his previous commitments."

Dan propped both hands on her desk and leaned in toward her. "Maddie, you are not a stupid woman. I refuse to believe that you are so dazzled that you don't realize he's using you."

She shrugged and dropped her gaze. "Maybe he is. But

it's not like I'm a victim. I'm willing to be used if that's what it takes to get his attention. I can't catch him with my looks, so maybe I can catch him with my ability."

Dan's normally cheerful expression turned fierce. He opened his mouth to argue just as the pizza deliveryman arrived.

"Anybody order pizza?"

They carried the large pepperoni pizza with extra cheese to the conference room. Dan flipped on the lights while Maddie rustled up some paper plates and napkins and a couple of sodas from the kitchen.

Maddie lifted the box lid and sniffed. "Yum. This looks like a feast."

Dan rested a hand on her arm. "Maddie, look, about earlier…"

She shook her head. "Topic closed. No point in spoiling a perfectly good pizza with an argument that nobody can win. Besides, I'm tired of talking about me." She sat at the table and after sliding a piece of pizza onto her plate, she scooted the box toward Dan. "I think it's time we decide what we're going to do about you."

He cocked a brow. "*Do* about me?"

"I was content to let you be an out-of-work photographer until I saw your work."

"I don't know how content you were," he muttered as he helped himself to the pizza. "You were busy trying to line up jobs for me."

"Be that as it may, it is now obvious you cannot continue in premature retirement. You are a phenomenally talented man. You can't let that talent go to waste."

"Yes I can. To borrow your word, I'm *phenomenally* tired of photography."

"How can you say that? You carry your camera with you everywhere. You should see how your face lights up when you pull it out and start shooting."

"Let me qualify my remark," Dan said. "I'm not tired of taking pictures, per se. I'm tired of my job in New York."

"I believe the term you used was *burned out*. Yes, I can see why working day in and day out with the most beautiful women in the world would get to you."

He frowned at the sarcasm in her voice. "No, you can't. But it's true. And they weren't beautiful. It's all an illusion. They are shallow, selfish people leading empty, meaningless lives. My job was to make those people look desirable so the rest of the world would want to be just like them."

"Is that a crime?"

His voice was hard, his eyes steely. "It's a crock. Think about it, Maddie. What kind of person dedicates their life to setting standards for beauty that are so high they can only be achieved by starvation and plastic surgery? Standards so unrealistic that normal, attractive people think of themselves as ugly."

She wanted to soothe away the anger and frustration she heard in his voice. "Tell me, where do you find beauty?"

He shrugged. "In normal people. In everyday things, like hands. Have you ever noticed the beauty of hands?"

Before she could respond to his question he caught her hand in his to study it. He turned it slightly, his fingers tracing tingly trails along her flesh.

"Your hands are beautiful," he was saying. "They speak of strength and compassion."

Maddie didn't know about the strength and compassion part but she did know he was stirring up some strange, delicious sensations as he stroked the sensitive skin of her palm.

Dan was on a roll. "I find beauty in eyes. Take yours," he said, his penetrating gaze holding her captive. "They are beautiful because of the size and color certainly, but more so because of the light that radiates from them. Your eyes are so expressive. You communicate volumes without ever saying a word."

She wondered what she was communicating right now. She pulled her hand from his to restore her equilibrium and ignored the blush burning her cheeks. "Then take pictures of those things. Eyes and hands, I mean. Other people's eyes and hands." Mercy, she was rambling.

"There's no market for pictures like that," he said, as a hint of bitterness crept into his voice. "People don't want reality, they want to see fashion models."

Until this moment she hadn't realized how disillusioned he was. "I'm sorry."

Dan laughed, but there was no humor in the sound. "I can't tell you how lousy it is to work so hard for something and then to come to the place in your life where you discover that everything you've worked for means nothing."

A long, thoughtful silence stretched between them. Finally, Maddie asked, "Do you have any money?"

Her question seemed to take him by surprise. "What?"

"I asked you if you have any money. Have you saved any of the undoubtedly extravagant fees you collected over the years?"

He shrugged. "Yeah. A boatload. Why?"

"Then marketability doesn't matter. You've got money. Enough that you don't have to worry about profitability, at least for a while. You need to do what feels right to you. The thing that feeds you."

"You're awfully wise this evening."

"It doesn't take a genius to know that it would be a crime to waste your talent. And if you decide taking pictures of everyday things isn't all it's cracked up to be, you've always got a safety net."

"What's that?"

She grinned. "Taking pictures of patio furniture, of course."

The mood lighter, they lingered over the pizza for a long time, laughing and swapping stories about the past. After they cleaned up, Dan hung around another hour to give Maddie time to finish up the presentation for Jack.

On the way down to the parking garage Dan said, "Oh, I almost forgot. I hope you were serious about keeping tomorrow open because I planned a little celebration in honor of your promotion."

Her heart did a happy little leap. A celebration for her? "You're kidding? That's so sweet. My day's wide open. What did you have in mind?"

"An early start. I'll pick you up at five-thirty."

Horrified, Maddie said, "Five-thirty? In the morning? Isn't that a bit early for celebrating?"

Dan chuckled. "I have a special place picked out. It takes a while to get there."

"I don't suppose you'd like to tell me where?"

"Absolutely not, it's a surprise."

The excitement of the celebration was slightly overshadowed by the prospect of an early start. She frowned. "Do activities held before sunrise qualify as surprises or nightmares?"

"Quit your griping. It's going to be fun."

"If you say so." She made no effort to disguise her disbelief. "What do I wear?"

"Something comfortable."

She unlocked her car and swung open the door. "Thanks for staying with me tonight. I appreciate the company."

"No problem. It was fun." He bent to brush a friendly kiss across her lips, as he had done the other night after dinner. "You'd best get on home. Tomorrow's going to start mighty early."

As she pulled out of the garage her thoughts were centered on the kiss. She knew Dan meant nothing by it; she suspected the sophisticated crowd he hung out with in New York exchanged casual kisses all the time, but that knowledge didn't stop her pulse from skittering when she remembered the gentle pressure of his mouth on hers. Mmmm. Kissing Dan was a habit she wouldn't mind developing.

Chapter Nine

Maddie stumbled out of the shower not much more awake than when she'd stumbled in. She squinted at the clock on the nightstand. It said 4:57 a.m. Yikes! Dan would be here in half an hour.

It took fifteen minutes to blow-dry her hair to the manageable damp stage and another five minutes to wrap it around her head. What a nuisance.

She'd been thinking about what Dan had said—that her father wouldn't want her to wear a hairstyle that made her miserable—and she'd come to the conclusion that he was right. Of course her dad would want her to be comfortable. She'd been thirteen when he'd told her he liked her long hair. If he were alive today he'd likely encourage her to wear a style more appropriate to an adult.

She was going to do it. She'd buy one of those hairstyle magazines from the checkout at the grocery store and pick out something that would look nice. Beneath the twinges of apprehension that went with the idea of change came the rock-solid belief that less hair, in any style, would be an improvement over her current furry-crown look.

She applied a couple of swipes of mascara to her lashes and a dab of lipstick. With just five minutes to spare, she stepped into her walk-in closet. Black skirts, black pants, black tops and black dresses lined the walls. She frowned. Seemed like a celebration called for something brighter. No point in wasting time wishing for what she didn't have. She grabbed a solid black tunic and a pair of wide-leg slacks.

She was slipping on her shoes when Dan rang the doorbell.

"Good morning," he said as he flashed her a wide smile.

Maddie's pulse did that skittery thing again and he hadn't even kissed her. Wow, he sure looked good in the morning.

"Good morning, yourself," she said. "Do you want to come in for a cup of coffee?"

"No time. We'll grab one on the way."

Maddie threw her tote bag over her shoulder and followed him out.

Dan drove through downtown Fort Worth, took a right at the Courthouse and pulled onto the highway heading east toward Dallas.

"We're not celebrating in Fort Worth?" Maddie asked.

"Nope."

"Where are we going?"

He shot her a grin. "Can't tell. It'd spoil the surprise."

"Aw, come on. How about just a little hint?"

He thought for a second. "Okay. I don't guess one hint would hurt. We're going to my friend's place."

Maddie was quiet while she thought that over. "Hmm. Your friend doesn't have a lake house does he? Because if he does, I didn't bring a bathing suit. Not that I own one."

"Why not?"

"Some things should not be unleashed upon mankind."

Dan rolled his eyes. "I should have seen that coming. But, to answer your question, no, my friend doesn't have a lake house."

"So where does he live?"

He shook his head. "No more hints. Sit back and enjoy the ride."

Maddie settled in to watch the scenery sail by. After twenty minutes she asked, "Are we almost there?"

"Sorta."

Have some dignity, she told herself. He obviously wasn't talking so she decided she wouldn't ask again if it killed her. She chewed her lip.

Her resolve disappeared when Dan turned into the DFW airport. "Your friend lives at the airport?"

"Hardly."

"Then why are we here?"

"Because we need to take a plane to get to his house."

"You're kidding, right?"

He wasn't kidding. He parked his truck in short-term parking and led her to the American Airlines Terminal. When their turn came at the ticket counter and he confirmed two first-class tickets to New York City all thoughts of dignity were gone.

"You're taking me to New York?" she squealed, loud enough to turn heads all over the terminal.

"Yeah. Just for the day. We'll hang out and go to dinner tonight then fly back."

"New York City for the day. Do you do this a lot?"

"Never. But we needed a special celebration for a special lady."

Maddie's heart melted. She threw her arms around his neck and kissed him smack on the mouth, right there in front of the ticket agent, all the passengers, God and everybody. It wasn't one of those sophisticated kisses Dan did so well, but Maddie's pulse jumped anyway. "You are the nicest friend in the whole world. I'll never forget this as long as I live."

He grinned. "Me, either."

Maddie had flown a couple of times in her life, but never first class. All traces of fatigue from her early-morning start vanished as they took their seats in the front cabin. She wanted to enjoy every minute of the adventure.

"I can't believe we're doing this," she said as she sipped excellent coffee from a porcelain cup. "Even my sister doesn't jaunt to New York for the day."

Maddie glanced at her watch. Seven-fifteen. Too early to use the phone in her seat to call her mother and do a little bragging. "My mother will flip when I tell her I went to New York City."

Dan grinned. "Have you ever been there before?"

"Never. But I've always wanted to go."

"I think you'll like it. We won't have much time but we'll try to hit a few of the hot spots. Being a woman you'll probably want to visit some of the stores."

She felt a familiar knot of dread in the pit of her stomach. She turned from him to look out the window. "I'm not much of a shopper."

"Then you obviously haven't been to the right places."

What would be the right place for her? Maddie wondered. Giants R Us? Maybe if she changed the subject he'd forget about shopping. "Do you miss the city?"

"Yes and no. There's an energy in New York that I've never experienced anywhere else. I never got tired of the fast pace. But I'm a Texan at heart. And it was time to come home."

"So how does a dyed-in-the-wool Texan end up in New York?"

He shrugged. "Looking for the next shot. I fell in love with photography as a kid. By the time I was eighteen I decided I was going to become a famous photographer. Everybody laughed at me. Even my own family thought I was nuts. They said that boys from Anawac weren't famous for anything but farming and livestock. I was just stubborn enough to pack up and move to New York City to prove them wrong. Once I was there I had to stay. I couldn't come home and listen to everybody say I told you so. Knowing I couldn't afford to fail kept me going through the lean times."

"It takes guts to leave family and friends to follow your dreams."

Dan wagged his head. "Boy, it almost sounds noble when you say it. You romantics sure know how to put a nice spin on things."

She chose to ignore his dismissal of her excellent reading of the situation. "You obviously went beyond the lean times. How did you break into the business?"

"I showed up at *Vogue* magazine one morning with my portfolio in hand. I told them I wanted to work for the best and since they were the best I wanted to work for them. No one's ever admitted it, but I think it was my Texas drawl and authentic beat-up cowboy boots that got their attention. I'm sure timing had a lot to do with it, but basically, I was a novelty."

Dan signaled the flight attendant for a refill on their coffee. "They sent me to Rick Fountain who was their premier photographer at the time. I 'gofered' for Rick for two years, you know—running out for coffee or picking up his dry cleaning. He paid me next to nothing. Panhandlers were in a higher tax bracket than I was. I think Rick expected me to pack it up and go home. When he figured out I wasn't giving up he started to take me seriously. He taught me the business. I was lucky. Rick is a genius."

"Were you two still working together when you quit?"

"No. He retired about five years ago. He bought a villa in Italy. He occasionally works the shows in Milan and we get together there."

"New York, Milan." Maddie sighed. "You've led the most exciting life."

"I'm glad one of us thinks so."

"What was it that soured you on fashion photography?"

He shrugged. "Nothing dramatic. Turns out fame wasn't much of a goal. Once I'd made a name for myself I realized it wasn't enough." He paused. "Have you ever stopped to ask yourself 'What am I doing with my life?'"

"Yeah."

"That's what I did. I took a long hard look at my life, my job, and I didn't like what I saw."

"So you quit?"

Dan nodded. "Rick taught me that an artist must invest himself completely in his work. When my heart was no longer in my photography I knew it was time to walk away."

Maddie's heart was in her throat. What amazing

strength it must have taken for Dan to turn his back on everything he'd worked for. She admired him for having the courage of his convictions and ached for him that his convictions had cost him so dearly.

In no time, the pilot was announcing their final approach into LaGuardia Airport. While Dan hailed a cab outside the baggage claim Maddie goggled. DFW was a busy world-class airport, but LaGuardia had something extra. Maybe it was that energy Dan had been talking about. Whatever it was, Maddie felt supercharged.

"Where to first?" she asked after they'd climbed into the cab.

"Like I told you, we're going to my friend's place."

She looked up from her search for a seat belt. "There really is a friend's place? I thought that was just a ruse."

"No ma'am, it's the real thing. And the first stop on our tour."

Dan gave their surly cabbie some instructions and they pulled away from the curb at warp speed. Dan laughed at Maddie's wide-eyed commentary of the trip. The people, the buildings, even the speed of the taxi were all covered with breathless excitement.

The cab reached Manhattan and screeched to a halt in front of a gray building, some twenty stories tall, indistinguishable from any of the others they'd passed.

Maddie craned her neck to see to the top. "Your friend lives here?"

"Works here," Dan corrected. "My friend owns the Renaissance Salon. He's a stylist. He's agreed to see you today as part of your pampering."

She swallowed a spurt of nerves. "What's he going to do to me?"

"As much or as little as you want. He's promised us one hour of his undivided attention. You can let him give you a new do or you can spend the time talking about the Mets' chances at the pennant this year. It's up to you."

Maddie's mind raced. This morning's adventure was taking on a whole new flavor. She'd been thinking about making a change. This was just the opportunity she'd been looking for. He could whack off her hair.

She grabbed Dan's arm. "Your friend—is he trustworthy? What I mean is, he won't make me look like a freak or something, will he? Purple spikes might make it in the Big Apple, but Cowtown is a tad more conservative."

Dan chuckled. "Thomas is pretty versatile. I know he's got a couple of rock star clients, but I also know he cuts the hair of some of New York society's blue bloods. I trust him implicitly. He won't steer you wrong."

Thomas's salon was a far cry from the ten-dollar flat-fee Cut Rate Hair Palace back home. The quietly opulent sixth-floor entrance said class and exclusivity. They stepped through the etched-glass double doors into a soothing oasis complete with piped-in harp music and a plant-bordered fountain.

Maddie slipped her hand into Dan's for moral support as they approached the superchic receptionist behind a mirrored desk.

"Hi. We've got an appointment with Thomas for ten."

"Dan Willis! I wondered who it was that worked the miracle of getting Thomas here before noon. I half expected European royalty." The receptionist smiled at Maddie. "Hi, I'm Suzanne. Welcome to the Renaissance. Would you like a latte?"

"Thanks, no. I drank three cups of coffee on the way here."

Suzanne grinned as she came out from behind the desk. "Then let me show you the ladies' room." As she led Maddie down the marble hall she called over her shoulder to Dan, "I'll return her to you in just a minute."

"So, how do you know Dan?" Suzanne asked Maddie.

"We work in the same office building. He's a friend."

"Have you known him long?"

"Not really. A couple of weeks."

Suzanne's brows shot up. "You must have made quite an impression on him. He called in a lot of markers to get you an appointment with Thomas. Thomas has a waiting list of three months. And he never works before noon."

Yikes. An appointment with a disgruntled, sleep-deprived stylist armed with sharp scissors didn't sound like an adventure. It sounded like disaster. "I hope he's not unhappy about fitting me in."

Suzanne dismissed Maddie's concern with a wave of her hand. "Are you kidding? He'd do anything for Dan. They go back a long way. Dan was the one who sent Thomas his first important clients. Dan has lots of contacts from his work with *Vogue*. Dan's referrals over the years have built this place. Thomas is only too happy to pay him back."

Suzanne pushed open another etched-glass door and stepped aside for Maddie to enter. "This is the ladies' lounge. Go ahead and slip into one of the smocks hanging on the rack over there. Just leave your clothes on the hanger."

Maddie glanced at the rack of emerald-green nylon smocks. Even if she hadn't known about the blue-blood clients and three-month waiting list she'd have known the

Renaissance was uptown. Anyplace that required a change of clothes for a haircut had to be first class.

"Can you find your way back to the front?" Suzanne asked.

"Sure. Thanks."

The shimmery green smocks were an unpleasant shock. Unlike the blousy long-sleeved smocks Maddie associated with berets and painting, these were cute little short-sleeved, wrap-around dresses cinched at the waist by a tiny tie belt. To make matters worse they appeared to come in "one size fits all." Every nearly six-foot-tall woman knows "one size fits all" is nothing more than a cruel joke.

Maddie's options were limited. She could refuse to wear a smock, which would make her look churlish after all the trouble everyone had gone through to accommodate her. She could pretend she misunderstood and wear the smock over her black outfit and make Dan look bad for having such a stupid friend. Or she could put on the miserable excuse for a robe, plaster a smile on her sure-to-be-beet-red face and brazen it out. She could almost hear her dad telling her to go for it.

She took her time getting dressed, hoping that by some miracle the tiny smock would expand. No such luck. Nearly naked, she peeked out of the lounge and looked up and down the hall for a sign of the receptionist. If Maddie could persuade Suzanne to take her directly to Thomas she would at least be spared the humiliation of having Dan see her like this.

The hall was deserted.

Go for it, Maddie. She sucked in a deep breath, stretched her mouth into a facsimile of a smile and walked down the hall in the direction she'd come from.

Dan leaned against the wall at the end of the hall, arms folded across his chest, waiting. At the sound of her footsteps he turned toward her and smiled. Suddenly his eyes widened and his smile faltered. "Maddie?" His voice was a wobbly octave higher.

She wanted to die. The smock fell at mid-thigh, exposing almost the entire length of her pasty white legs. After seeing the shock on his face she glanced over her shoulder, considering bolting back to the ladies' room.

Too late. Dan walked slowly toward her, his gaze making a thorough study of her overexposed body. "Your legs, Maddie. They are gorgeous."

Busy trying to formulate a witty remark to cover her acute embarrassment, she missed the compliment. "Oh, well," she said with a manufactured laugh. "We can't all be runway models."

His hands clamped down on her shoulders and he looked her straight in the eyes. "I said, your legs are *gorgeous*."

She didn't know what to say. Afraid he'd just complimented her to cover his initial shock, she said, "That's nice of you to say so."

At the moment Dan didn't look nice. He looked mad. The pressure of his hands on her shoulders tightened. "Why do you do it?"

"Do what?"

"Sabotage yourself?"

She didn't pretend to misunderstand him. "I'm not sabotaging anything," she said, her anger climbing to meet his. "I'm protecting myself. I know what I look like, Dan. I see myself in the mirror every day. I'm big. But that doesn't mean I have to advertise it."

Just that quickly the anger was gone. He shook his head. "Oh, Maddie, I wish you could see yourself through my eyes."

"I'm not sure *you* can see through your eyes if my big white legs look good to you. If you must know the truth, I don't know how you made a living with your bad eyesight."

He refused to take the bait. "Will you let me tell you what these eyes see?"

She swiveled her head to look at the hands pinning her. "I doubt you'll let me go until you do."

"Smart girl." He released her then and took two steps backward. He folded his arms and studied her so intently she could swear she felt the heat of his gaze.

"I see long legs with creamy smooth skin that tempts me to touch." The throaty whisper felt like a caress.

Maddie snorted, partly to cover her embarrassment, partly to still the sudden quivering in her stomach.

He raised a hand for quiet. "I see the shapely legs of a woman, not the spindly legs of a colt or a malnourished model. You have very sexy legs with mouth-watering curves. And your ankles…"

Wow. Maddie didn't think she could take any more. She was just a degree or two shy of melting point, and if he whispered something about her ankles she'd probably dissolve into a quivering puddle.

"Hi, Maddie," Suzanne chirped from behind Dan. "They're ready to take you in for your facial and shampoo."

Maddie couldn't move.

"Go ahead," Dan said, his voice low. "I'll be waiting."

Chapter Ten

Dan accepted a cold drink from Suzanne, not sure whether he should drink it or douse himself with it. Whew. He swiped at the beads of perspiration on his lip.

He'd been completely unprepared for the sight of Maddie in that short little smock. For a second there in the hall he had felt like he'd been tossed headfirst into a blast furnace.

He'd been stunned. He'd known she had legs of course; it stood to reason there was something beneath all those layers of black fabric. But he'd never expected them to be great legs.

He shifted in his chair and swallowed hard. Really great legs.

There was a lot more and less to Maddie than met the eye, even a trained eye like his. She'd really pulled one over on him. On everyone. She wasn't dumpy. She was amazing.

The shapeless clothes she favored added twenty or thirty imaginary pounds to her tall frame. What a shock to discover she had a waist and that her arms and legs were toned and shapely.

Maddie wasn't the willowy type. She was womanly the way Dan thought women ought to be. Strong and healthy with luscious curves and intriguing shadows.

Dan drank deeply to relieve his suddenly dry mouth. Maddie had some killer curves.

He wished he'd handled the whole thing differently. Letting his jaw drop to the floor when he first saw her was stupid. Worse, he knew Maddie mistook his response for horror. Then to cap it all off, he accused her of sabotaging herself. Very stupid.

He'd spoken in anger. He wasn't angry with Maddie but with her family, who had raised her to believe she was a giant. He was angry with a world that set such a narrow definition of beauty, then worshipped it above all things.

And he was angry with himself. As a fashion photographer he bore the guilt of supplying unrealistic images as the standard for beauty.

Thomas swept into the reception room on a burst of energy. "I'm here before noon, Suzanne, just as I promised. Alert the media."

"Hi, Thomas. Dan and Maddie are here. Maddie went back for her facial and shampoo about an hour ago, so she's due at your chair any minute."

Thomas turned to zero in on Dan. His face split in a wide grin as he hurried toward him with outstretched arms. "Dan, my friend, welcome home."

Thomas was an interesting combination of elegance and flamboyance. He looked as if he belonged on stage.

An inch or two over six feet with mahogany skin and bleached blond hair, Thomas always dressed in severe black. He needed only a whirling satin-lined cape and silk top hat to complete the image of magician.

Dan stood to embrace him. "I really appreciate you doing this for me."

Thomas batted the remark away. "Are you kidding? It's my pleasure. Now tell me, how have you been?"

Other than Maddie, Thomas was the only person Dan could be completely honest with. "Out of focus. Trying to figure out what to do with my life."

Thomas frowned. "Still in career limbo?"

"For now."

"New York misses you. Every model that walks through those doors bemoans the loss of the great Dan. You could write your own ticket if you came back."

Dan shook his head. "No thanks. I may not be clear on what I want to do, but I'm dead sure about what I don't want to do. No more fashion photography."

"You keep saying that, but I can't picture you without a camera in your hands."

"Me, either." Dan shrugged off the dark image of life without his pictures. "A friend recently suggested I forget fashion and just take pictures of what I like. I'm not sure what I'd do with them, but I might give it a try."

"As long as it makes you happy I'm not worried. Everything you touch turns to gold."

"I appreciate the vote of confidence."

Thomas motioned with his chin toward his station. "Suzanne says your friend should be ready by now. I don't want to keep her waiting. Come on back with me. We can visit while I work."

Dan's nerves gave a nasty jolt. Even now he wondered if he'd made a mistake in bringing Maddie here. Was it hypocritical to hate the focus on external beauty and then go to extraordinary measures to achieve it? In hauling Maddie to the finest stylist in New York City was he practicing the very thing he preached against?

He'd been locked in a wrestling match with his conscience since he'd first made the call to New York. He believed a person needed to make peace with who they were—to accept their own unique beauty. On the other hand if a person had no idea they possessed any beauty, wasn't it his responsibility to point it out? Was it wrong to bring unrecognized beauty into focus?

He didn't have the answer. His only consolation was that his motives were pure. Maddie was the first true beauty he'd met in a long time. As far as he was concerned, she didn't need a makeover to shine. But if a makeover would open her eyes to her own beauty then nothing was too good for her.

Dan fell into step alongside Thomas. "About my friend. She's not like the others I've sent you."

"You mentioned she wasn't a model."

"No—"

Thomas chuckled. "Don't try to tell me she isn't beautiful. I'll never believe that you've lost your touch with women or that your impeccable taste has changed since you went south. Remember, I know you too well."

What could he say to Thomas that wasn't disloyal to Maddie? "She's beautiful, but not in the ordinary way." Dan stopped, taking Thomas's arm to force him to a halt as well. "She's fragile. I know she doesn't look it, but she is."

"Relax. I'll handle her with kid gloves."

Even with that reassurance Dan felt uneasy. He sent up a silent prayer that Thomas would be on his best behavior. He loved the man like a brother but he also knew Thomas could be cruel. More than once he had carved up a snotty overblown beauty with his razor-sharp tongue.

It was a risk Dan would have to take. He had seen the incredible power of transformation in Thomas's hands. The man was a genius with an unerring eye for the perfect hairstyle for a face. If anyone was up to the challenge of Maddie's sleeping badger hair, it was Thomas.

Maddie waited in Thomas's styling chair. With her freshly shampooed hair wrapped in a turban on top of her head and her face glowing from the facial, she looked like the standard salon work in progress. A scared work in progress. Her normally large eyes grew larger still when Thomas swept into the room.

"So you are the remarkable woman who has caught Dan's eye." Thomas took her hand and lifted it to his mouth for a kiss. "Good morning, Maddie. I'm Thomas."

Maddie was clearly impressed with the continental greeting. "Hi. Thank you so much for agreeing to see me."

"It's my pleasure." He stepped behind her chair to face her reflection in the floor-to-ceiling, gilt-framed mirror. "What can I do for you today?"

"If you have time, I'd like you to cut my hair."

"I always have time for a beautiful woman." He unwrapped the turban, letting the mass of hair trail over her shoulders and down the back of the chair. "Tell me about yourself."

"There's not a whole lot to tell."

"I'm sure there is. But first you must relax." Thomas

gently massaged her shoulders as he eased her back into the chair.

Though her back now touched the chair, Dan didn't think she looked any more relaxed. Her posture said scared rabbit ready to bolt.

"Dan says you're from Fort Worth. Have you lived there all your life?" Thomas carefully combed through her hair as she answered. It was so long he had to crank the chair up to its highest position to comfortably reach the ends.

Dan could see Thomas sizing up Maddie as he listened to her talk about her job and home. Dan knew he would study her bone structure, the shape of her face, the texture of her hair, even her personality before deciding on a style.

"Your hair is amazing," Thomas said. "It has a life of its own."

Maddie grimaced. "I know."

Thomas frowned at her reflection. "Why do you say it like you are ashamed? Your hair is beautiful and thick. It has so much body."

"It's like wearing a jungle. I feel like it's smothering me."

Thomas smiled at her. "That's because there is too much. Too much of anything wonderful, even chocolate or champagne, is no good."

Dan's brows shot up. This was a day of surprises. He'd had no idea his friend possessed so much tact. Or such a gift of understatement. To say Maddie had too much hair was like calling the Grand Canyon a ditch.

Thomas continued to comb. "Do you have a hairstyle in mind?"

"Not really. Just less hair."

Thomas nodded. "I'd like to go much shorter. To your chin, if you'll let me."

Dan saw alarm flash across her face. She obviously hadn't anticipated such a radical change. Maddie glanced over at Dan, looking for his input. He sent up another frantic prayer that Thomas wouldn't fail them, then winked at Maddie.

She met Thomas's gaze in the mirror. "Okay."

Dan saw Maddie gulp as the first twelve-inch strand hit the floor. He knew how she felt. His stomach felt the way it did at the first long drop of a roller coaster. So much was riding on this appointment. Thomas wasn't just cutting her hair. He was issuing her a ticket to self-confidence.

Minutes ticked by as lock after lock dropped to the floor. Thomas chattered away while he worked, as though he weren't aware of the nerve-charged atmosphere. When he finally put down his scissors, her still-damp hair hung in waves even with her chin.

Maddie slanted an excited grin to Dan. Dan took his first easy breath since he'd entered the room. He smiled at Maddie and gave her the thumbs-up sign.

Thomas turned to Dan. "I'm going to blow her out. Do you mind running to get us something to drink?"

"Sure. No problem."

Dan hobbled out on stiff legs. He'd been sitting there for over an hour, too frightened to move for fear of distracting the master at work.

When he returned with tall icy glasses in tow, Thomas was just finishing up. He swiveled the chair around to face the mirror and met Maddie's eyes in the glass. "So what do you think?"

"Omigosh."

Omigosh was right. Even knowing Thomas was the best, Dan hadn't expected anything like this. Maddie's thick dark hair, now parted on the side, curled in sexy waves around her face. The length emphasized the size of her eyes, the height of her cheekbones and the fullness of her lips.

Dan was fully focused on those lips when they turned up in a smile.

"I love it," she told Thomas. She shook her head from side to side. "I feel a hundred pounds lighter."

"Are you interested in losing another two pounds?" he asked.

Uh-oh. Thomas's supply of tact and good behavior had suddenly run out. Two pounds of hair could mean only one thing. The eyebrows. Dan shoved a glass at him and another at Maddie in an attempt to change the subject. "You two must be thirsty. Drink up."

The distraction failed. Maddie leaned out of her chair and looked around Dan to ask Thomas, "What do you mean?"

"Your brows."

Dan should have seen it coming. Why hadn't he warned Thomas to stick to hairstyles? Poor sensitive Maddie was sure to think nothing about her was good enough. "She's fine—"

Thomas simply talked over him. "They're too heavy for your new style. Less hair—less brows."

Maddie didn't bat an eyelash. "Can you fix them?"

"No, but my assistant can. She's a brow guru. Let me call her. I'll call the nail technician while I'm at it. She can give you a pedicure at the same time."

Thomas made a quick call and almost immediately a purple-haired young woman in a lab coat arrived to escort Maddie down the hall. As Dan stood to follow them, Thomas caught his arm. "Why didn't you tell me?"

Dan's eyes were on Maddie. "Tell you what?"

"That you're in love with her."

Dan's head snapped back toward Thomas. "Don't talk crazy. Me? In love with Maddie?" He laughed. "No way. We're just friends."

"I've got a newsflash for you. Friends don't look at friends like you look at Maddie." Thomas was enjoying Dan's discomfort. "You're in love. Admit it."

"Look, if I was in love, I'd know it. I wouldn't need anybody to tell me."

Thomas laughed as he clapped Dan on the back. "Whatever you say, man. Just be sure to invite me to the wedding."

An hour and a half later Maddie met Dan in the reception area with tears rolling down her face.

Dan shot out of his chair and covered the room in three long strides. "What's the matter?" he asked, taking hold of her shoulders to look into her eyes. "Did they hurt you?"

She shook her head.

"What is it, honey? Did somebody say something to you?"

She nodded.

Dan stiffened, rage burning in the pit of his stomach. "Just tell me who it was—"

She placed a hand on his chest. "A woman stopped me in the ladies' lounge just now," she said with a sniffle. "A Ricki Somebody. She says she knows you. She heard that I was here with you and she wanted to know if we were in town doing a shoot."

Dan was completely bewildered. "I don't understand. Why are you upset? Was she nasty to you?"

Maddie smiled through a new wave of tears. "She thinks I'm a model."

The watery explanation didn't help. He was still confused. "And that makes you sad? I'm sure she meant it as a compliment."

Now she was beaming. "I'm not sad. I'm happy."

Whew. Dan's shoulders relaxed as the need to pound somebody evaporated. "If this is happy, I'd hate to see sad."

He pulled a tissue from a box on a nearby table and gently dabbed at her tears.

She pulled back in alarm. "Don't wipe off my makeup."

"Would it upset you to know there's nothing left?"

She laughed. "Oh, well, I can try to redo it. The makeup artist was amazing. She taught me all kinds of tricks. I bought the stuff she used so I could do it at home. Speaking of which, I'd better settle up my bill."

"What bill? You're my guest."

Maddie frowned as she reached into her tote bag to pull out her wallet. "That's nice of you, but I couldn't possibly let you pay for all of this. I'm sure it cost a fortune."

Dan laid his hand on her arm in gentle restraint. "You're worth it. Consider it a little something to celebrate your promotion."

Fresh tears spilled down her cheeks. She leaned toward him, kissing him lightly on the cheek. "Thank you, Dan. This is better than Christmas or my birthday or even my promotion. This is the very best day of my life."

Now she was going to make him cry. He picked up a fresh tissue to blot her face. "It's not over yet. We've got some time before we have to be back at the airport. It's not every day you get to New York City. Is there something special you'd like to do?"

She thought for a moment. "Something touristy."

"Okay. How about we do the Staten Island Ferry? A trip out to the Statue of Liberty is on the top of every good tourist's list."

She looked at him as though he'd suggested she kiss a snake. "What? Stand on the deck of a boat and mess up my hair? You've got to be kidding."

Dan laughed. "Spoken like a true model. Okay, let me think. Something touristy that doesn't involve moisture and wind. How about the Empire State Building? It's another must-see destination for tourists, and you'll be far away from water, although it is a bit breezy on the observation deck."

"Define a bit breezy."

"Well under hurricane force."

"Empire State Building, huh?" She worried her bottom lip with her finger. "It might be neat to see the city from there."

He forced his gaze from her mouth. "You could call your mother from the top. She'd be totally impressed."

Maddie grinned. "Okay, that settles it. I don't get to impress my mother very often. I guess it's worth risking the breeze."

"Excellent. I've said my goodbyes to everyone, so we can go."

Maddie shook her head. "Give me a minute to fix my makeup."

The light in her eyes and radiance of her face couldn't be improved by cosmetics. She glowed. But he wouldn't cheat her out of the opportunity to do the female thing. He waited while she primped and powdered in front of the mirror for several minutes. "Come on, glamour puss. You look great. Let's go."

Chapter Eleven

Maddie knew Dan was the kind of guy who'd say she looked great even if she didn't, but at this moment she truly felt great. For the first time in her life she felt almost beautiful. Until she glanced down at her heavy black pants and matching tunic. Yuck. Add to the gloomy picture her flat black shoes that resembled matching pontoons and she was a poster child for frumpy.

This morning in Fort Worth the outfit had been not too great. Here in New York with her gorgeous new hairdo, it was just plain awful. Instead of saying "Best Day of My Life," the outfit screamed "Frumpy Matron From Hell."

"I feel like Cinderella with only half her wishes granted."

Dan frowned. "What's the matter?"

"My clothes," she said, plucking at the fabric of her pants.

"No problem. We'll go shopping. I know some terrific shops. We can stop on the way to the Empire State Building."

The self-doubt that had been miraculously absent all morning now surfaced. Shopping was always a disaster for her. It would be so much worse to have Dan witness her inevitable humiliation. No point in ruining the perfect day with a cruel dose of reality. "I don't think so. I'm not much of a shopper."

"Whatever you say." He reached out, taking her hand in his. "Come on, the Big Apple is waiting."

The subway ride was more exciting than the flight. She loved it. She loved climbing down the long flights of stairs into what felt like the bowels of the earth. She loved the smells—some good, some not so good, but all imprinted in her memory.

She loved the bright unnatural glow of the tunnel lights far beneath the city skyscrapers. The sounds of the people were as fascinating as the squeal and hiss of machinery.

She didn't want to waste the experience sitting along one of the seats that lined the car. She and Dan stood, sharing a pole in the aisle. When he winked at her and closed a hand over hers to steady her as the subway swayed and jolted its way through the tunnel, she knew she'd never been happier.

The view from the top of the Empire State Building was spectacular. Even without the binocular-like contraptions set up for the tourists, she could see for miles. She leaned on the railing to stare out over the city. Her heart soared like the cotton clouds. She was Queen for the Day, on top of the world.

"I've got to call my mother." Maddie rooted through her tote bag to find her cell phone. She punched in her mother's number and listened to the rings, praying she'd be home. Even a call from the top of the world would lose some of its impact on an answering machine.

"Hello?"

"Hi, Mom, it's me."

Dan smiled and moved a discreet distance away when he saw the call had gone through.

"Madelyn, where are you? I called your apartment this morning and you didn't answer."

"I couldn't," Maddie crowed. "I'm in New York."

"You're where?"

She'd done it. She'd impressed her mother. "I'm in New York City. I flew up this morning with a friend to get my hair cut and do a little sightseeing. At this very moment I'm standing on top of the Empire State Building—"

Her mother cut her off, "I remember when your sister went to the Empire State Building. It was four or five years ago…I think it was the year she and Steve attended that plastic surgeons' convention in New York. Don't you remember? They stayed at the Plaza. Jennifer was very impressed. Are you staying overnight? You really ought to see if there's room at the Plaza."

Maddie felt like a balloon with a slow leak. "No. We're coming back tonight."

"Too bad. Oh well, have a wonderful time. Call me tomorrow and tell me all about it. I'm going to your sister's after church and I'm not sure when I'll be home. You better call me there."

"Okay, I will. Goodbye."

Maddie clicked off the phone and dropped it back into her bag.

"That was quick," Dan said, strolling back toward her. "Did you tell her about your hair?"

"I mentioned it."

"Was she surprised to hear you were in New York?"

"Not really. My sister was up here a couple of years ago."

Though he didn't say so, Dan seemed to sense her disappointment. "Where to next? We've got an hour or so to kill before I take you to dinner at this great little French place. My friend owns it. I called him while you were doing the beauty thing and told him we were coming. He's looking forward to meeting you."

"I didn't bring anything to wear."

"You look fine."

No, she looked like a refugee. She wasn't about to meet Dan's friend looking like last week's laundry. "You mentioned some shops earlier." It pained her to say it. "Do you think they would have anything to fit me?"

"Since you have no deformity, no extra head or limb that would require special accommodations, I must assume you are referring to your height."

"Yes. It's…" How to describe her bleak shopping experiences without sounding pitiful? "It's hard to find things that fit."

He looped his arm through hers and guided her back toward the elevators. "That's only because you don't know where to look. I, on the other hand, know the best places."

Maddie was skeptical. "How's that?"

"Think about it. I've been working with women for the last twelve years. Models. They're all at least five-foot-ten. At least."

She hated to state the obvious, but he just wasn't getting it. "It's not just the height. I probably weigh more than half a dozen of your models put together."

He waited until they'd stepped off the crowded elevator into the lobby, then he stopped her, placed his hands firmly on her shoulders and impaled her with his eyes. "You are tall, not large. Do you hear me? I'm not sure where you ever got the warped idea that you are anything less than perfect unless it was from hanging around your under-sized mother and sister."

When she rolled her eyes and tried to pull away he tightened his grip. "I've seen you, Maddie. You may try to hide the truth from everybody else, but I've seen you and you are magnificent."

Magnificent. Like a work of art or a valued treasure. She teared up again, right there in the middle of the lobby with New Yorkers and tourists pressed in on all sides.

"Aw, honey," Dan dug in his pocket for a tissue he'd had the foresight to pick up at Renaissance. "I didn't mean to upset you. I just want you to hear the truth. You've got to accept yourself for who you are."

She brushed away the tears with the back of her hands and blew her nose in the tissue he'd produced from his back pocket. "Okay, I'll try."

Dan kissed her on the forehead. "That's my girl."

In order to save time, Maddie and Dan took a cab from the Empire State Building to the store. The shop Dan selected wasn't situated in a long row of department stores on Fifth Avenue as Maddie had envisioned, but was tucked away on a side street. From the outside, the shop looked tiny. One look at the ultra-chic mannequins in the store window and Maddie was ready to run.

"I don't know, Dan," she said, hanging back. "This doesn't look like the kind of place that has anything for me."

"What? Do you have X-ray vision to see what's inside from out here?"

She got only a glimpse of the name of the store, Valerie's or something, before he mercilessly dragged her through the front door.

The storekeeper hurried toward them. "Dan! How are you?" She hugged him. "When did you get into town?"

"Just here for the day. I brought Maddie to do some sightseeing. She's from Fort Worth."

He stepped back and extended an arm for Maddie to join them. "Maddie, let me introduce you to Tonia. She owns the shop."

Maddie and the owner exchanged greetings.

"What can I do for you today?"

Maddie liked her immediately. First, because she was at least an inch taller than Maddie and every bit as big, but secondly because she was kind enough not to take one look at Maddie's awful outfit and throw up her hands in despair. "Dan and I are going out to dinner and I didn't bring anything to wear."

Dan mentioned the name of the restaurant to give Tonia some idea of the dress code.

Tonia looked Maddie over. "You could wear what you have on. Black's a good color on you. You might want to throw on a belt to dress up the outfit a bit."

Belt? Yikes! Maddie didn't do belts. Her mother had warned her away from them years ago. Think how embarrassing it would be if Tonia didn't have one in a size to fit. Too late. Tonia was already speeding toward a rack with a selection of leather and chain belts.

"Let me show you what I have." She pulled several from the rack and before Maddie could protest fastened one around her waist. It was wide black leather, and rather than cinch her waist, Tonia hooked it so it hung at a cocky angle above her hips.

Tonia stepped back to consider the effect. "I like it. What do you think?"

Maddie was speechless. She was wearing a belt and it looked good. Really good. It even made her frumpy out-fit look half stylish.

Tonia was already on to other things. "Now if you want something completely different, I've got a couple of dresses that will look great on you."

A couple? As in more than one? This was too good to be true.

"Do you have a favorite color?" Tonia asked. "I'd suggest jewel tones. Strong hues will really play up your coloring."

"She looks great in emerald green," Dan said with a teasing grin.

Tonia pulled four or five garments off the rack and carried them to a curtained dressing room at the far end of the shop. "See what you think of these."

Maddie had to force herself into the dressing room. Things had been so positive up to this point, she didn't want to spoil it by discovering that nothing fit.

"Come out and model when you have them on," Dan said. "We can help you decide."

She shot him a smile that was mostly gritted teeth. As nice as Dan was, there was no way she was leaving the dressing room in anything too tight, too small or too short. Since Tonia had never asked Maddie her size, and Maddie had no intention of volunteering it, there were bound to be some misfits.

She undressed slowly.

"What's taking so long in there?" Dan griped. "Do I need to come in and speed things along?"

She had no doubt he'd do it. Maddie yanked off her top and pants and dropped the first dress over her head. The dressing room had no mirrors so Maddie was forced to go out to see how it looked.

"Wow, Maddie." Dan whistled long and low. "Knock-out."

Tonia bustled forward to smooth down the skirt in the back. "It's a good look for you. Strong. Not fussy, but feminine."

The dress was blue, the same royal blue as the sundress she'd admired at the mall. It flowed down her body to just below her knee in a tailored column of silk.

"It really plays up your figure," Tonia said. "You've got a great bust."

Dan was quick to agree. "I couldn't have said it better myself."

Maddie ran her hands along the delicious fabric. It looked good. It felt good. The dress was gorgeous. The rich color and lines were miles away from her usual style. "I don't know. Do you think it's too tight?"

Dan shot to his feet. "No!"

Tonia glared at Dan then turned to Maddie. "Not at all. Tight is counting your ribs or reading the brand name in the elastic of your panties. Tight looks like the wearer is trying too hard. This fits well. It follows your curves. It's body-conscious."

"Uh-huh." Dan's enthusiastic reply was accompanied with two thumbs way up. "And what a body."

Maddie looked from Dan then back to her reflection. "I'll take it."

They stayed an hour. Maddie bought everything Tonia brought to the dressing room plus a few extra items she couldn't live without. Like a pair of black "body-conscious" slacks Tonia assured her would mix and match with the pieces she had at home, two belts, a snug white T-shirt that made Dan's eyes glaze over and a three-inch silver cuff bracelet that reminded Maddie of a superhero.

Her very favorite purchase of all was a sundress Maddie stumbled across almost by accident. Crafted of rich rosy gauze it fell in flirty folds to Maddie's calves. This was her dream dress—the one that said cool, confident and sexy. After her makeover today, Maddie could almost believe she was all three.

Maddie tried not to flinch as Tonia tallied up her purchases. The twenty-five percent discount she got for being Dan's friend brought the total down from unspeakable to outrageous. Still, she handed over her credit card without a second thought. The clothes were fabulous and with any luck she'd bought enough that she wouldn't have to shop again for a year.

Tonia handed them the bags and they said their goodbyes. Outside Dan said, "One more stop before we go to eat."

"Where to?"

He walked to the curb to hail a taxi. "Bloomingdales."

Maddie frowned. "More shopping?"

"A beautiful dress deserves beautiful shoes."

She stuck out a foot. "I've already got a perfectly good pair of shoes."

"Your shoes are good but we're looking for great. I can't say I understand it exactly but I've worked with enough women to know that there is some sort of mystical power in a pair of really great shoes."

As much as she hated to shop she had to admit that her

pontoons lacked mystical power. Nor did serviceable flat black shoes do anything to enhance the look of the sleeveless emerald silk dress she'd chosen to wear for dinner. "One pair."

Bloomingdales's shoe department was amazing. The sheer volume of styles boggled Maddie's mind. "I have no idea where to start."

"I do." Dan picked up a pair of strappy black sandals. "Try these."

She shook her head. "I can't wear those. Look at that heel. I'll look like Godzilla." She glanced down at her dress. "Or the Jolly Green Giant."

He pressed them into her hands. "Try them."

"Bully."

By the time the salesman made his way over and asked if he could help, Dan had selected three more pairs of shoes for her to try on. And none of them were flats.

"Dan," she hissed when the salesman left to find the shoes in her size. "I can't wear heels."

"I disagree. Unless they are uncomfortable, you should wear heels."

That made it easy. All she had to do was claim discomfort and she could have her flats.

The salesman bustled out with a stack of boxes. The box on top was the pair of black sandals. He helped her slip them on. "How do they feel?"

Maddie stood, expecting to hit her head on the twenty-foot ceiling. Not even close. She didn't even get a nosebleed. She took a few experimental steps. They felt okay. She couldn't run a marathon in them, but since she wasn't a runner, it was a moot point.

"Go look at yourself in the mirror," Dan instructed.

She strolled to the mirror without a single wobble. She looked down at her reflection. The shoes looked great. They even made her feet look smaller.

Dan joined her. She noted that even with heels she wasn't taller than him. They stood eye to eye.

Not that he was looking at her face. Dan was studying her legs. "Notice how the heel accentuates your slim ankles and the curve of your calves?"

He had that glazed-eye look again. And he was speaking in that throaty whisper. The same one he'd used when she'd stepped out in the smock.

"I'm getting the feeling you must be a leg man," she joked to cut through the sudden tension.

He rubbed a hand over his face. "I don't know about that, but I think I'm beginning to understand the mystical power thing."

Maddie thought she did, too. She bought three of the four pairs.

Before they left Bloomingdales they stopped in the luggage department to buy something to carry home all of her purchases. The clerk helped them stow her new clothes and shoe boxes in a large suitcase with a telescoping handle and wheels.

Outside Bloomingdales they hailed another cab. Maddie patted the suitcase on the seat beside her. "I've never carried a suitcase into a restaurant before."

"Are you kidding?" Dan picked up her black tote bag. "This suitcase goes everywhere you go."

Embarrassed, she tugged it from his hands. "It's a tad big I suppose, but it's a proportion thing."

"Be serious. You'd have to be King Kong to be proportionate with that bag."

"You don't like it?"

His expression softened. "It's not that. The bag is fine. What I don't like is the thinking process behind the bag. The one that makes you believe you're a giant. The one that makes you buy bulky clothes and flat shoes to camouflage the real you."

She stared at her lap. "You think I'm sabotaging myself."

He took her hand and waited for her to look up at him. "I'm sorry I said that. It was dumb. I was angry because you think beauty only comes in size two. You're a beautiful woman. It's time for you to see that."

Dan leaned forward to instruct the cabbie. "Pull over. We'll get out here."

After Dan paid the driver and he and Maddie stood out on the sidewalk in front of an apartment building, Maddie said, "This doesn't look like a restaurant."

"It's not. The restaurant is two blocks south. I thought I'd get a few pictures of you before I lose the light. Okay?"

She could hardly say no to a man who'd indulged her every whim. "Why not?"

"Excellent." He whipped his camera out of his ever-present camera bag.

"What do you want me to do?"

"Just walk," he said. "I'll get what I need."

Self-consciousness and new shoes made her gait feel awkward, as though she was swishing her hips back and forth. She felt silly pulling her new suitcase down the sidewalk.

Dan wasn't complaining. "Beautiful. Beautiful."

He was behind her, then beside her, then in front of her snapping away the entire time. They'd walked a block when he stopped to reload.

An old woman sat at the top of a short flight of concrete stairs leading up to one of the apartments. Maddie had seen her watching them walk down the block.

"You can take my picture," the woman offered.

Dan looked up at her and grinned. "Thanks. I'd like that."

Maddie waited at the base of the stairs and watched Dan. The minute the camera went to his eye he was completely absorbed in his work. He shot several pictures of the woman from different angles. Other than the wrinkled model, Maddie imagined this was what it would be like to see Dan in action.

There was something very sexy about Dan behind a camera. His moves were purposeful, his concentration absolute. A sense of focus and complete control seemed to emanate from his body. She never imagined that watching genius in action could pack such a physical punch.

When he was finished he climbed the stairs to the woman's side and offered his hand. "I'm Dan Willis."

She shook his hand. "Cordelia Tamayo."

"It's nice to meet you, Cordelia. I got some excellent pictures of you. If you give me your name and address I'll mail you copies."

Maddie hurried up the stairs to supply her with a pen and piece of paper.

"I hope you don't think I give my name out to just anyone," Cordelia said with a coy smile as she handed him the information. "At my age I've become very selective. I'm only giving it to you because you're cute."

Dan laughed.

"I bet you couldn't tell I'm eighty-six years old."

"No ma'am. I wouldn't have put you a day past seventy."

Cordelia giggled. "Go on now. You and your pretty lady have more things to do than to stand here talking to me."

He glanced at his watch. "We do have to move on. We have reservations for dinner."

"Goodbye. And don't forget to send me my pictures."

"I won't." Dan grabbed Maddie's hand. "Come on pretty lady. Time to eat."

They walked the next block, stopping in front of a canopied door. A uniformed doorman ushered them inside. Maddie blinked to adjust from the fading daylight to the candlelit interior.

"Welcome, Mr. Willis. We have a table ready for you. Right this way."

The sommelier appeared instantly at their linen-draped table. "Would you like a bottle of wine this evening?"

"No wine," Dan said. "Tonight is a special night. The pretty lady and I would like a bottle of champagne."

Dan selected something off the wine list and the obviously pleased sommelier hurried off to get it. "I'm starving," Dan told Maddie.

She peered at him over the top of her menu. "Poor thing. Haven't you had anything since breakfast on the plane?"

"I ate a couple of those frou-frou sandwiches they serve at the Renaissance, but two tiny round sandwiches aren't enough fuel for shopping and sightseeing."

"I was too nervous to eat the sandwiches," Maddie confessed.

"I'm sorry. You should have said something. I've been running your legs off all day. We could have skipped the shopping and come straight here."

"Are you kidding? I wouldn't have missed it for the

world. I have a whole new beautiful wardrobe courtesy of Tonia. Throw in a new hairstyle and some eye shadow and I'm a new woman."

"I hope not. I liked the old Maddie. The clothes are beautiful, but make no mistake. You are beautiful without them."

Maddie's brows shot up.

Dan grinned. "Must have been a Freudian slip. What I meant was the clothes are nothing more than a pretty frame for a work of art."

The sommelier returned with the champagne and two glasses. He performed the opening and serving of the champagne as though it were a sacred ritual.

After he had left, Dan lifted his glass in a toast. "To Maddie, a true work of art."

It was almost embarrassing to drink to such lavish praise. Maddie sipped the champagne then raised her glass. "To Dan, whose poor eyesight adds tremendous value to the art."

He was unamused; his glass remained on the table.

She tried again. "Okay, how about this? To Dan, the author of the very best day of my life, my dear fairy godfather and friend."

"I can drink to that."

Dinner was delicious. Dan ordered several different dishes so she could sample the specialties of the house. Half a dozen times Maddie was tempted to pinch herself. She was living a page in a fairy tale.

Here she was in New York City, dining in an elegant candlelit restaurant with the handsomest man—wait! Dan wasn't the handsomest man, Colton was. Funny, she hadn't thought of Colton all day.

Not once had his golden face intruded in her fantasy—not even when she'd bought the little sundress for the reunion. Odd that pleasing Colton's palate hadn't entered her mind the entire time she'd been at the salon or trying on clothes.

Each time she had stepped from the dressing room she had watched Dan's expression. When his brows tipped up and his dark eyes grew darker still she'd known she had a winner. Dan's opinion mattered most.

Candlelight flickered on Dan's face. He smiled and her pulse did the skittery thing. Maybe she'd been too hasty in pegging Colton as the man of her dreams.

They lingered long after dinner, talking and laughing. Dan introduced his friend, the owner, who clapped Dan on the back and complimented him on his good taste in women. Several other friends stopped by the table to greet Dan and ask him if he were back for good.

Each time, Dan shook his head. "No, I'm happy in Texas."

One speaker looked at Maddie and nodded. "I can understand why."

When they'd finished dessert and the last drop of champagne, Dan looked at his watch. "My dear, your carriage is about to turn into a pumpkin. It's time to go home."

Maddie hated to leave. She didn't want her fairy-tale day to end.

They caught a cab to LaGuardia and after checking her suitcase, boarded their plane. The early-morning start seemed to catch up with Maddie as they taxied down the runway for home.

"Tired?" Dan asked.

She nodded. "But I don't want to go to sleep. I don't want to miss anything."

He flipped up the armrest between them, wrapped his arm around her shoulders, and pulled her close. "Go ahead and sleep. I promise I'll wake you if anything exciting happens."

It was so easy to rest her head on his strong shoulder. Cradled under his arm Maddie had the strangest sensation of coming home. She closed her eyes and slept.

Four hours later they were standing in front of her apartment. "Dan, I can't begin to thank you for today."

"No thanks are necessary. I had a great time."

"You're wrong. Thanks are vital. You've done so much for me."

He grinned. "Yeah, I helped you max out your credit card."

"Be serious," she said, biting back a smile. "What's a lifetime of debt to the incredible thrill of a new wardrobe and three pairs of shoes? I'll be the talk of the office on Monday."

She didn't think he looked very pleased. His grin faded as he said, "I'm afraid you're right."

"I appreciate everything you've done for me. You have to be the nicest man in the world."

She leaned closer to kiss him lightly on the mouth. In a split second his arms came around her in a velvet vise. He pulled her to him and kissed her hard. When she would have pulled away, he moved toward her and deepened the kiss. His mouth moved on hers, teasing and demanding, drawing her into a haze of passion. This was no friendly peck. This was…wow!

Suddenly he pulled back, his hands on her shoulders to steady her as she swayed toward him. "No, Maddie." He sounded almost angry. "I'm not a nice man."

Maddie slumped against her closed front door after Dan

left, unsure that her legs would carry her. What was that? How had a chaste goodnight peck between friends at the door transformed into a mind-melting embrace? And why did it feel so right?

Chapter Twelve

Monday morning, Maddie's courage failed at the critical juncture. Just two steps past her front door she freaked. What was she doing? She couldn't go to work looking like this.

She told herself the blue silk was too dressy for Monday at the office but the unvarnished truth was, she was scared. She wasn't ready for the attention a new hairstyle, new makeup and clothes would attract.

What if it looked like she was trying too hard? What if instead of pretty she looked pitiful? What would they be saying about her in the ladies' room? Poor Maddie looks like the Beast in party clothes? She couldn't bear to think people would be laughing behind her back.

She rooted in her tote bag for the apartment key. She wasn't being a coward, she told herself. She was just breaking her new look in by degrees.

She hurried inside and slipped off her dress. She paused

to admire the beautiful color and fabric before rehanging it carefully. Next stop, the sink. She scrubbed off the makeup she'd awakened an hour early to apply. For today she'd stick with her old faithful lipgloss. Finally she headed back to the closet. As she reached for a long black dress she thought of Dan. He'd gone to so much trouble for her, she knew he expected to see her in something new today.

She could tell him she'd decided the new dresses were too dressy for a Monday, but she knew he'd recognize cowardice when he saw it. He'd be so disappointed in her. Hadn't she promised to stop hiding behind big clothes? To play up her assets and take pleasure in who she was?

She compromised with a mixture of old and new. She wore one of her old black blazers over her new white T-shirt and her "body-conscious" black pants. She wore heels, not because Dan expected it, but because for some crazy reason they made her feel powerful. As a finishing touch she clamped on her silver superhero bracelet.

Satisfied that she wouldn't be a laughingstock, she headed to the office.

The first person she met at Cue was Jack. She joined him at the front door and they walked in together.

"Hi, Maddie." He cocked his gray head and smiled. "You cut your hair. It looks nice."

There, she thought, that wasn't so bad. Maybe she'd blown the whole makeover thing out of proportion. "Thanks."

"Did you and Dan have fun Friday night?"

"Yeah. We didn't do much. Ate pizza and laughed."

He stopped at the door of his office and smiled. "Sometimes those are the best dates of all."

"It wasn't a date. We're just friends." Her face heated as she thought of their "friendly" kiss outside her door.

"Ahhh." Jack didn't look or sound convinced. "For what it's worth, I liked him. Seems like a nice guy. Tell him I was serious about putting him to work. We always need photographers."

The idea of asking a world-famous photographer to take pictures of lawn furniture brought a smile to her lips. "I don't think he'll be able to work for Cue. He's found a job."

"So soon?"

"He's really talented, Jack. Someday when we have more time I'll tell you about it."

"Maddie! Is that you? I love your hair!" Crystal's squeal carried the length of the hall. Within seconds four or five women crowded around Maddie to see what all the fuss was about.

"You didn't say anything about getting it cut. Where did you go?"

All eyes were on her. Maddie tensed, waiting for an off-hand dig or a shared look of pity. Nobody laughed. They seemed genuinely pleased for her.

"I got it done in New York," Maddie said. "Thomas at the Renaissance cut it for me."

"You flew to New York to have your hair done?"

Maddie bumped from Beast to celebrity on the merit of a haircut.

She'd worked all her life to be accepted. Since being big wasn't acceptable she'd tried everything to hide her size. She'd been desperate to fit in. She would never have believed it if someone had told her all it took was an out-of-town hair appointment.

She was still the main topic of discussion as the staff gathered half an hour later in the conference room for the Monday morning meeting.

Colton was late arriving. "Hi, Maddie," he said, pressing through the group to her side. "Were you able to get the presentation finished?"

"She's been busy," Crystal told him. "She flew to New York City to get her hair done."

Colton looked at Maddie. "You cut your hair. It looks nice."

Jack called the meeting to order, effectively ending all private conversations. "We can talk later," Colton said before he moved away to take a seat.

The meeting flew by. After Jack dismissed them, Maddie walked back to her office on cloud nine, her yellow legal pad clutched to her heart.

Nobody laughed. They thought she looked nice. And when Colton spoke to her in the conference room, he looked at her. Really looked at her. Eyes focused and everything.

She didn't stop at the ladies' room. No point in chancing it. Wasn't there an old saying that eavesdroppers never heard anything good about themselves?

Maddie put in a full morning at her computer. She answered mail and polished up the information she'd compiled Friday night on Electronics Era for the meeting with Jack. One-hundred-percent immersed in the presentation, she was surprised to glance at her watch and see it was eleven-thirty. Her pulse jumped. Lunchtime.

She couldn't wait to see Dan. They hadn't talked since their universe-shifting kiss on Saturday night. She needed to see his face, to read in his eyes and hear in his voice whether things had changed for him.

It was possible the kiss meant nothing more to him than "Good night. I had a nice time." For Maddie, it had changed everything.

Coming on the heels of a day of discovery, the kiss seemed to open her eyes to the truth. She was head over heels in love with Dan.

Or at least she thought she was.

The problem with being a hopeless romantic was her tendency to read too much into a situation. Case in point: could a person determine the depth of their feelings for another based on a single kiss? Maybe she wasn't in love at all. Maybe what she was feeling was an acute case of gratitude with a generous dollop of lust.

She'd spent nearly every waking moment since then trying to sort out her feelings. She was grateful to Dan. She was attracted to Dan. Was it love? Her thoughts were tangled like thread.

In the end she decided that between the two of them, Dan was the levelheaded one. Since she was afraid to trust her own feelings, she'd take her cues from him as to how to proceed.

She pulled out her nifty new compact and dusted a little powder on her nose. She applied some of the lipstick the makeup artist had assured her would make her lips irresistible. Maddie wasn't foolish enough to believe marketing hype, but if shiny lips could win her a kiss from Dan like the last one, she was all for it.

Dan saw her arrive in the cafeteria and waved her over to his table when she'd gone through the line. Nerves jangling, she approached the table slowly, watching for signs of what he was thinking in his face. His wide smile told her nothing.

"Hi, beautiful." He pulled out her chair and took her tray so she could settle in. "How'd it go this morning?"

His voice sounded different. Breathless. Was it possible he was nervous, too? "Rave reviews, just as you predicted. I think they liked my hair, but the fact that I went all the way to New York to have it cut pushed me over the top. The Beast has become a woman of mystery."

Dan laughed.

"The only real problem I foresee is maintaining my celebrity status," she said, only half teasing. "How do I top this when the novelty of the haircut wears off?"

"How about a facial in San Francisco?" Dan suggested. "Or perhaps a pedicure in Paris?"

Maddie chuckled. "Maybe a massage in Milan."

The silliness seemed to clear the air. As they laughed, Maddie's revved senses idled back to normal.

"I'm proud of you, Maddie. For someone who avoids the spotlight, it must have been tough marching into the office this morning."

"Don't be too proud. I didn't march. I slunk. I lost my nerve big-time as I was leaving my apartment and ended up running back inside to change. If it wasn't for the absolute certainty that you'd be disappointed in me, I'd have showed up for work in something big and black."

He took her hand, his tender smile causing her heart to melt. "This isn't about me, Maddie. What I like, what I want is immaterial. You have to do what makes you feel confident. It's all about you."

Their eyes met and for a moment nothing existed for Maddie except the two of them. She was so wrapped up in Dan, she didn't see Colton approach.

"Any room at the table for me?" he asked.

When Maddie didn't immediately respond Dan said, "Sure. Sit down."

Colton placed his salad on the table and his empty tray on an adjacent table. "I'm Colton Hartley," he said, extending a hand to Dan.

"Dan Willis."

Colton poured dressing over the top of his salad and picked up his fork. "What do you do, Dan?"

"I'm a photographer."

Maddie finally found her tongue. "Dan's from New York. He's—"

"—out of work," Dan finished for her, while sending her a smile that said leave it alone.

"That's too bad. Maybe something will turn up."

Maddie heard the dismissive tone in Colton's voice. It wasn't snotty or an obvious put-down, but she'd been around him often enough to recognize the subtle cooling.

Colton was the kind of guy that backed a winner. Not that she was ready to accuse him of snobbery. She suspected that someone who had it all simply couldn't relate to anyone who didn't. She wondered why Dan would allow Colton to draw such an erroneous conclusion. She knew for a fact Dan was not a loser. He was amazing.

Colton turned his attention to her. "So Maddie, talk to me about Electronics Era. Were you able to get anything done over the weekend?"

"I hope so," Dan said with a pointed look at Colton. "She was here past midnight working on it.

"I feel really badly about that. It's just that it came up so last-minute and I had plans—"

Dan nodded. "That's just what I told Maddie. That she shouldn't let a last-minute deal interfere with her plans.

But you know Maddie, company woman to the core. She'd rather break our date than drop the ball."

"Our date?" Maddie asked.

"Not that I'm complaining," Dan hurried on before Maddie could speak. "Any time with Maddie is a great time." He capped off the outrageous remark with an infatuated grin.

Maddie glared at him as though he'd lost his mind.

Colton's remorse appeared genuine. "Look, I'm really sorry."

"It's not a problem. I wanted to do it," Maddie said for the benefit of both men.

Dan looked at Colton. "What did I tell you? Company woman to the core."

Whatever Dan was trying to pull, Maddie was ready to change the subject. "I think you'll like the direction I went with our ideas for Electronics Era, Colton. I dropped the brand name roll call completely and placed full emphasis on store selection and staff expertise. I believe with time we can erase their tacky image."

"Where do you see the print campaign going?"

The conversation took off from there. With Dan acting as a sounding board, Maddie and Colton tossed ideas back and forth. Maddie thought Dan provided some excellent input. Of course, knowing his background it made sense he understood the mechanics of product image.

"I feel like we're ready to go to Jack with this." Colton said before turning to Dan. "You know, you seem to have a natural aptitude for advertising. You might want to look into it since the photography thing isn't panning out."

Dan's mouth turned up in a wry grin. "Thanks. Maybe I'll do that."

Colton checked his watch. "Maddie, are you ready to get back? We can catch Jack and show him what we've got."

Maddie cast one final look at Dan's untouched chocolate cream pie before turning to Colton. "I guess we should."

Dan rose with them. "You two head back to work. I think I'll stick around a while longer. I've got a piece of pie to finish." He tapped the plate for emphasis.

Colton missed the gloating look Dan sent Maddie. "It was great to meet you, Dan. And I meant what I said about your knack for advertising. If you decide to start looking around I'd be glad to supply you with some names."

Dan watched them wind their way through the maze of occupied tables until they were out of sight. He was surprised by the sick feeling in the pit of his stomach at the sight of Colton walking at Maddie's side.

They looked like they were enjoying each other. Wasn't that what Maddie wanted? To capture the elusive attention of the great Colton Hartley.

Dan sat, scooted the piece of pie in front of him and picked up one of the two forks. He'd chosen the dessert with Maddie in mind. Chocolate seemed to be her favorite. He could tell by her longing glances she'd been dying to dig in, but she hadn't. Not with Mr. Perfect looking on.

And he *was* perfect. Sitting directly across the table from Colton gave Dan ample opportunity to find flaws in Maddie's idol. And he'd given it his best shot. He'd scrutinized Colton's face as though he was looking through a camera lens.

Colton's thick blond waves showed no sign of receding. Although Dan had detected contacts, they didn't appear to be tinted; Colton's sky-blue eyes were the real thing. His coloring, complexion and bone structure needed no touch-up. His teeth had to be veneers but Dan didn't think he could count that as a flaw. Broad shoulders and a killer physique completed the picture.

Physically, the guy was perfect. No wonder Maddie was ga-ga for him.

Dan put down his fork, the pie untouched.

Of course, there was much more to a man than looks. Personality, intelligence and character were the true measure of a man, but could any flesh-and-blood woman see beyond the movie-star looks and thousand-watt smile to the flawed man inside?

Not many. Dan's experience said most people looked at the outside. Period. But then, Maddie wasn't most people. As one who'd been judged harshly for her looks, she of all people had learned to value people for their inner beauty. Wasn't that one of the first things that had attracted him to her?

Dan picked up the fork again. Maddie was an intelligent person. She knew that Colton was a cocky and self-absorbed credit thief. She'd experienced firsthand his selfishness.

Unfortunately, as much as he'd like to, Dan couldn't paint Colton as a complete villain. He did seem to have a thin streak of nice down the middle of all that ego. Maddie couldn't have missed his offer to supply Dan with names to help him find a job.

Dan resisted the urge to panic. Maddie could handle it. He smiled as he remembered the horrified look on her face when he'd bragged about her in front of Colton. Or when he'd said their date had been interrupted. She might be content to let Colton ignore her, but Dan wasn't. It was time somebody told Colton how great and desirable Maddie was, if he was too stupid to see it for himself. It made Dan sick to see how Colton devalued a woman who was worth more than he would ever be.

She'd walked into the cafeteria that morning like a woman who believed in herself. For the first time since he'd known her she'd walked with her shoulders back and her chin high, carrying her nearly six feet of height with pride. He wasn't going to let Colton, with his innate superiority, rob her of that.

Chapter Thirteen

Maddie pushed open the door of Dan's office and stepped inside. Dan sat, kicked back, his cowboy-booted heels propped on the desk.

"Where were you today?" she asked. If her voice sounded snippy it was because she was feeling that way. She'd been looking forward to seeing him all morning.

"I was just going to ask you the same thing." Dan sounded a little cranky, too.

She let the door swing closed behind her. "I was in the cafeteria."

"So was I. Usual place. I don't know how I missed you."

The knowledge he'd been looking for her brought a smile to her face. "I got down there late. Colton and I were in a meeting until twelve-thirty. It was probably another fifteen minutes before we got to the cafeteria."

Dan's brows shot up. "We? Colton was with you? Again?"

"Yeah, can you believe it?"

He swung his feet off the desk and onto the floor. "No, I can't. That's what—five days in a row now? What will his harem say?"

"I'm sure they were none too pleased, although it was just a working lunch. Come to think of it, I did feel some murderous glares when we sat down."

"Better watch your back."

Maddie laughed. "What's all that?" she asked as she focused on the stacks of black-and-white photographs on the desk.

Dan shrugged. "Some pictures I've taken."

"May I?" she asked, reaching toward one of the piles.

"Why not?"

She picked up the top photograph. It was the old woman they'd met in New York. "Hey, this is Cordelia."

"Yeah. I got a couple of good shots of her."

Maddie studied the pictures. "They're lovely."

"Thanks."

Maddie frowned. "*Lovely*'s not really the right word."

"I don't know. I liked it."

She gave him a playful shove. "What I mean is, it doesn't begin to cover what I'm feeling. The actual composition is lovely, the placement of Cordelia in relation to the stairs and railing is aesthetically pleasing, but it's so much more than that. This picture hits me on an emotional level."

Maddie flipped through several more shots, studying each of the images. "It's weird but when I look at these I don't see individual elements like lighting or location. All the components add up to a feeling. They're very powerful. I feel like I know these people just from looking at their pictures."

He reached up to flick the ends of her hair. "That's the romantic in you. You have a great imagination."

"No. You have a great talent." She propped her hip on the desk and picked up another stack of pictures. The subjects were varied. There were children and adults, some shots of the whole person and some where only a face or hand filled the frame. Maddie didn't know how long she sat studying the shots.

When she'd looked at the last one she squared off the stack and laid it on the desk. She moved slowly to allow her churning emotions to normalize.

It took her a long time to find her voice. "Your pictures aren't what I expected."

Dan adopted a stricken expression. "Uh-oh."

"I'm serious. With black-and-white photography I expect starkness. Most I've seen are hard, almost bleak, the kind that leave you feeling empty and alone. But yours are different. There is an empathy in each picture you take. I can't explain it but I get a feeling of connection with each of your subjects. As though I am linked to them by some invisible cord."

He grinned. "I think that's good."

"Dan, these are fabulous. You have the ability to breath life into a photograph."

"Did I tell you my middle name is Frankenstein?"

She rested a palm on his chest and locked eyes with him. "Be serious. You have a tremendous gift. You've got to share it."

He waved at the desktop. "Take what you like."

She swatted his hand. "Stop kidding around. I'm talking about going public. I think you need to do a show."

"Thank you."

"It's not a compliment. It's a sacred trust."

His grin faded. "I don't know, Maddie. I'm glad that you enjoy them, but as far as anybody else—"

"I didn't enjoy them," she corrected. "I was moved by them. I experienced them. And others will want to, too."

"I'm a fashion photographer. No one would take me seriously."

Maddie folded her arms across her chest and studied him for a long moment. He had incredible talent. Did he honestly think he could turn his back on his amazing gift? He might be ready to throw in the towel but she wasn't about to let his genius go to waste. Maybe he just needed a little push. "I don't blame you for being afraid," she said.

He stiffened, a muscle working in his jaw. "This has nothing to do with fear. I'm being realistic."

She knew she'd made him mad but she refused to back down. "Aren't you the one who is constantly hammering me to believe in myself?"

"This is entirely different."

"Not at all. It all boils down to fear of rejection."

Dan's chin lifted a fraction. "I'm not afraid."

Wisdom told her she'd pushed him far enough. For now. "Okay, I won't bug you any more. But I want you to think about what I've said. Your talent is too amazing to keep to yourself." She glanced over at the clock radio on the corner of his desk. "Oops. I'm supposed to be back at Cue."

Dan hopped up from his chair to walk her to the door. "Hey, since we missed lunch today, how about dinner tonight? If we feel wild we can throw in a movie."

"I'd love to, but I can't. Colton and I are taking a client out to dinner."

Dan frowned. "Isn't that going above and beyond the call of duty?"

"It was Jack's idea. He thinks the client feels neglected. Colton prescribed wining and dining them."

"That would be Colton's specialty," Dan muttered.

"Don't be tacky. Any face-to-face time with a client is good business. I'm glad you took me to New York. My suddenly busy social calendar is putting a real strain on my wardrobe."

He brightened. "No problem. We can run up to New York tomorrow and hit the stores."

"Cross-country shopping sprees two weekends in a row? Wouldn't that give the girls in the office something to talk about?" She sighed. "I wish I could, but we're shooting our Electronics Era spots tomorrow."

Dan's frown was back. " 'We' being you and Colton?"

"Yeah. We don't do the actual filming, of course. But since we're the account team we've got to be there."

"What's the deal? You two have been practically inseparable this week."

Maddie chuckled. "We've earned a new nickname at the office. I heard Crystal call Colton and I the Dynamic Duo."

Dan didn't appear to appreciate the humor. "Swell."

Maddie frowned. "For somebody who was pretty hot under the collar about Beauty and the Beast, you don't seem particularly happy about my upgraded title."

Instantly contrite, he took her hand. "I am. Really. I guess I'm still kinda wrapped up in the whole 'what do I want to be when I grow up' thing. Sorry. I'm happy things are going so well for you."

He walked back to the desk and slid open the top drawer. He sorted through a stack of business cards, extracting one from the pile. "Here's Tonia's card. Give her a call. She'd be happy to ship you whatever you need."

Maddie took the card. "Valkyrie? The name of the shop is Valkyrie?"

"So?"

Maddie laughed. "Isn't that the name of the warrior women from Norse mythology?"

"I guess so. Why, what's so funny?"

"I couldn't figure out why all the clothes in her shop fit me. It's because she caters to Amazons."

"Not Amazons. Women over five foot ten. I sent a lot of models to her."

Maddie waited for the rush of shame that always followed a discussion of her size. It didn't come. He didn't see anything abnormal about her size. Why should she?

Dan came around the desk. "If you're working tonight and tomorrow, that pretty much shoots the weekend. What have you got going on Sunday?"

"I'm heading to Dallas for church and lunch with my mother and my sister and her family."

"I'm not doing anything. I'd be glad to tag along if you need moral support or a character witness."

She shook her head. "Tempting offer, but I'd better pass. Spending an afternoon with family carries the mandatory sentence of fawning over my niece and nephew and listening with awed admiration as my mother recounts each of Jennifer's incredible accomplishments. Truly cruel and unusual punishment. I couldn't do it to you."

He shrugged. "I don't have anything better to do."

"You're sweet, but I couldn't subject a friend to such torture. I'll have to go it alone."

"Whatever you say."

He looked so disappointed it was on the tip of her tongue to beg him to come with her, but she stopped herself before the words could slip out. Their relationship was new and fragile. She didn't want to risk exposing him to a dose of her family's "Maddie is a loser" mentality.

"Trust me, you'll have an opportunity to spend time with the whole motley crew real soon. You haven't forgotten your promise to pinch hit at the reunion, have you?"

His smile didn't pack the usual punch. "You're on the calendar."

"Great." She put her hand on the doorknob. "I've got to get back to work."

"I imagine Colton is frantic, wondering where you are."

Maddie chuckled. "Not likely. He's not just another gorgeous face, you know. He's plenty capable without me. But I do think he's beginning to appreciate me. His eyes don't glaze over any more when I talk to him. I think he might actually be listening."

"He'd listen if he had half the sense you say he has."

"I think he does. Our styles are so different, but instead of clashing, they seem to complement each other. We make a really good team."

"Swell."

Dan stood at his door long after Maddie left. Ever since Colton had begun to figure prominently in Maddie's life, not as an unattainable dream, but as an actual physical presence, Dan had felt as though he had a continuous case of the stomach flu. And if the sight of Maddie and Colton together made him queasy, then the idea of them being dubbed the Dynamic Duo made him want to puke.

If she was going to be paired with anyone, it was going to be *him*. Not that Dan was making any progress in that direction. She'd been so busy with work they hadn't had time to talk about what had happened between them. The few times they'd been alone, Maddie had shown no indication of wanting to be a couple. If anything, she seemed to have pulled back.

The kiss at her door had been a mistake. He'd meant to keep it light but when she'd told him for the millionth time that he was a nice man, he hadn't been able to take it any more. He wasn't motivated by niceness. He wasn't a saint. He was in love.

It had all happened so fast, Dan hadn't understood his feelings for Maddie until Thomas had pointed it out for him. Once he put a label on his feelings, everything fell into place. Crazy but true. He'd fallen in love with her the very first time they met.

Filled to overflowing with the exciting discovery, Dan had kissed her with his whole heart. Big mistake. He'd obviously frightened her with his passion. And no wonder. If she thought about him at all, it was as a friend. She'd probably pulled back from Dan as a gentle reminder that Colton was the man of her dreams. And now, the man of her reality.

In the week since he and Maddie had flown to New York, Colton had joined them for lunch every day. Sure, most of the conversation had centered around business, but, for crying out loud, did they have to do it on Dan's time?

Dan was jealous. He was sick of seeing Colton's too-good-looking face in the picture. Worse, he hated the thought that he might have been the one to stir Colton's interest in Maddie. After all, Dan had been the one to catalog Maddie's fine points. He feared he'd done too good of a sales job. His intention had been to show Colton that Maddie was every bit as good as him, not to convince Colton to add her to his stable.

Lately Dan's hope that Maddie would see beyond Colton's exterior to the true man inside had dimmed. The man had dazzled her. She couldn't say enough nice things about her partner.

Wouldn't it be ironic if the empty beauty that had driven Dan from the job he loved was the same force that now lured the woman he loved away from him?

Chapter Fourteen

"Okay people, let's walk through this one more time before we shoot it." The director led the actors to the edge of the store's television department where they would open the commercial, made a few staging suggestions, and signaled them to begin.

PJ Platt, the owner of Electronics Era, bustled up to Maddie, who stood just outside the ring of cables and lights to watch the progress.

"I hope this is almost finished," he said, loud enough for everyone in the room to hear. "The store opens in forty minutes."

"Yes, sir," she whispered back. "They'll be rolling the film in less than five minutes. If all goes well and we don't have any more interruptions, we'll have the equipment packed up and out before you unlock the doors."

If he heard her pointed remark about interruptions, he didn't acknowledge it. "What if it doesn't go well?"

"Then your customers will have the opportunity to witness a real commercial being made."

Her clipped response didn't leave much room for discussion. "Oh. That's not how we planned it," PJ said, "but I guess it wouldn't be so bad. Might bring some business."

As PJ hurried away to annoy someone else, Colton appeared at her side. "I don't know how you put up with that guy," he whispered in her ear.

"I don't have any choice," she whispered back through gritted teeth. "Every time he shows up, you disappear."

Colton grinned to acknowledge she'd figured out his strategy. "You're better with the whole 'hand-holding' thing than I am."

Maddie's brow shot up. "Don't sell yourself short, Colton. I'm sure you're a world-class hand-holder when the incentive is right."

His smile widened. "You might be right." He turned to follow PJ's progress through the crowd. "I don't know what it is about the guy, but every time he makes a suggestion, I want to strangle him."

"You'd have to take a number," she said. If anyone had earned the privilege of strangling their client, it was her.

PJ Platt had shown up at 7:00 a.m. sharp, along with the film crew, actors and team from Cue. No problem there. It was not uncommon for company representatives to attend a shoot. Having been in on the creation of the commercial from the beginning, many clients enjoyed seeing the concept come to life. The understanding was that at this point they would be spectators only.

Not so PJ. Caught up in the Hollywood spirit, he'd interrupted the process a half-dozen times to interject comments and suggestions. Most were simply superfluous; some were downright stupid. All of them delayed filming.

Maddie saw early on that if they were to maintain peace on the set, it was up to her. She'd done her best to serve as a buffer between PJ and the production crew. Since no blood had been spilled, she felt she'd been successful.

"Quiet, please," the director said. "We're ready to roll cameras."

Maddie sprinted to PJ's side, snagged his arm and half carried him toward the employees' lounge. "Come on, PJ. It's been a long morning. Let me buy you a cup of coffee."

"But they're filming," he protested, while looking back over his shoulder toward the set.

"Right. And that's why we're leaving."

He gave her a blank stare.

She couldn't very well say he wasn't welcome in his own store, so she lied. "It's bad luck for a client to be present on the first take."

"Oh. I had no idea."

Maddie dragged out their coffee break through three takes. She was wondering how much longer she could hold out when Colton popped his head into the break room and said, "That's a wrap."

PJ looked crestfallen. "I missed everything."

"Just the boring stuff." Colton clapped him on the back. "You might want to run out there now and talk with the actors before they go."

PJ bolted for the door.

Maddie flopped back in her chair. "Whew. I'm glad that's over. If I drank one more cup of coffee, I swear I'd float away."

"Hmm. I guess I'd better reword my invitation."

"What invitation?"

"I thought we might grab a cup of coffee when we finish up here, but under the circumstances I think I'll change it to an invitation for brunch. Hungry?"

"Starved."

They brunched at a trendy little spot downtown. Though it wasn't quite noon, it was already ninety degrees out, so they passed up the umbrellaed tables outside and sat inside in the air-conditioning.

Colton greeted half a dozen friends, mostly conspicuously salivating women, on their short trek to the window-side table. Conscious of the envious scrutiny she received because she was with Colton, Maddie was careful to suck in her stomach and roll her shoulders back as she walked by his side. Funny, being the object of envy brought so little pleasure. For Maddie it seemed only to increase the uncomfortable pressure to measure up.

The waitress arrived immediately. After the customary three-second delay it took any red-blooded woman to find her voice after coming face-to-face with Colton's beauty, she asked, "Can I start you two off with coffee?"

"None for me, thanks," said Maddie. "Just water. In a very small glass."

Colton chuckled. "Coffee for me."

The waitress hurried away to do his bidding.

"I think the shoot went well this morning," Colton said.

Maddie nodded. "The raw footage looked good. It's such a step up from anything Electronics Era has done before. Dare I say classy? I believe PJ will be pleased."

"I liked the way you handled him."

"No, you liked the fact that I handled him so you wouldn't have to."

He had the good grace to look sheepish. "That, too. You did a nice job. Very subtle."

"You must have missed the part when I got him in a headlock and threatened to punch out his lights if he said another word," she teased.

Colton laughed. "I was talking about the finesse you used to keep him out of the way. Very smooth. If you ever get tired of advertising, I think you have a real future in the diplomatic corps."

She knew he was kidding around, but there was genuine admiration in his eyes. "Thanks."

The waitress returned with their drinks. "Are you ready to order?"

Maddie had worked up a major appetite riding herd on PJ. She could cheerfully down a stack of pancakes with a side of eggs and bacon. But not with Colton watching. "I'd like a bran muffin with a side order of fresh fruit, please."

"Bring me the same."

The waitress flashed Colton a you-can-have-anything-you-want smile and disappeared.

Maddie glanced out the window. The streets were quiet on weekends. A couple strolled by, hand in hand. Maddie smiled, thinking of Dan holding her hand as he showed her New York City. What a wonderful day that had been.

"What's the smile for?" Colton asked, the expression on his face showing that he assumed it was for him. Being Colton, that would be a pretty safe bet.

She wondered what he'd say if she admitted she'd been thinking about another man. She'd be willing to wager he'd never heard those words. "No special reason."

He watched her a moment. "You're different."

Oh, for heaven's sakes, had he just now noticed? And here she'd been telling herself he'd actually been looking at her. "Yeah. I cut my hair."

"No, it's not the hair. You've changed."

"How so?"

"I don't know. You seem more aware of yourself as a woman."

She hadn't thought about it before, but he was probably right. The leading authority on woman would know those things.

Whether she was different or not, he was certainly looking at her differently. This was not the way he looked at Maddie the co-worker whose name escaped him. This was not even the way he looked at Maddie his valued partner. No, this was more of the look he saved for size-two beauties. The one that said, "Yum yum, I like what I see."

"I—I hadn't thought about it," she stammered.

His deep voice deepened and he turned the full power of his blue gaze upon her. "Whatever it is, it's very attractive."

She broke eye contact. "Thanks."

"Didn't you say something about a family thing coming up?"

She nodded, her eyes still trained on the silverware. "I have a family reunion next Saturday."

"I don't know if your invitation still stands, but I've discovered an opening in my schedule on Saturday."

She looked up to see if he was serious. He looked sincere. Sincerely on the make. "Hmm," she said. "Let me get back to you on that."

An outraged scream echoed through Maddie's sub-conscious. What was she doing? Why was she hesitating? The Red Sea was parting and she was standing on the edge, deliberating over whether or not she was ready to cross. This was nuts. Colton, the god, had just volunteered to take Maddie, the giant, to the family reunion.

She didn't have to bribe him or drug him or kidnap him. He *wanted* to go. She was living her dearest dream. And she told him she'd get back to him? Wake up girl! What was there to think about?

Dan.

Her dear friend now figured prominently in the fantasies that had once featured Colton. The warmth of Dan's touch, the fire in his gaze, the passion in his kiss—these were the things filling Maddie's thoughts and crowding Colton from her mind.

Dan was perfect. He might not be Colton's equiva-lent in looks—what mortal was?—but he stood heads above Colton in the things that mattered. Dan was a perfect friend, perfect gentleman, perfect kisser. If he had one fault it was his imperfect eyesight and how could she count that as a flaw when he thought she was beautiful?

She hadn't told him how she felt. She'd been afraid. At first she was afraid that she'd romanticized gratitude and lust into love. Then, even after she was sure her feelings ran deeper, that she truly loved him, she'd kept quiet. She was afraid to expose her heart. It was diffi-cult to speak up when she'd spent most of her life hid-ing who she was and how she felt. It was time for a change.

She needed to talk to Dan.

Once she knew what she had to do, Maddie was on pins and needles. She must have smiled and conversed with Colton while she ate her meager meal, but by the time she got to her car she couldn't remember a single detail of their brunch.

She raced up to her apartment and dialed Dan's number.

"Hello?"

"Hi, Dan."

"Maddie? What's up? I thought you were off shooting commercials today."

She could hear the smile in his voice. The one that said he was glad she'd called. "I was. We finished up before eleven."

"That was quick. I was about to run out for some lunch. Are you hungry?"

"No, Colton and I went out for brunch after the shoot."

"Oh." His voice went flat. "The Dynamic Duo strikes again."

"Something like that. You're never going to believe this but Colton asked if he could go to the reunion with me."

After a long pause Dan said, "He did? That's great. I had hoped something would work out."

Definitely not the answer she expected. "I thought you wanted to go to the reunion."

"Me? No. I offered to help out if you were in a bind, but this is good. I've been planning to do some traveling. Now that I don't have to worry about the reunion I'm free to go."

Maddie sat down hard. "I didn't know you were planning a trip."

"It's kind of last minute. Actually, the idea came from you."

"I don't remember telling you to go away."

"I bet you remember telling me it's a crime to waste talent and that I should think about doing a show."

"Yeah, but I thought you could use the pictures you have."

"Maybe. Honestly, I don't even know if I want to do a show. I'm hoping that a trip will help clear my head. And I might get some pictures I can use if I decide I want to do an exhibition."

Maddie felt panicky. Everything was slipping away, like water leaking through cupped hands. "How long will you be gone?"

"Hard to say. As long as it takes."

This wasn't going the way she'd planned. She wanted to talk about how much they meant to each other. She wanted to tell him she loved him. "It won't be the same when you're gone."

"You can handle it."

There didn't seem to be anything left to say. "Call me when you get back."

"Yeah, sure."

Chapter Fifteen

Maddie met her mother in the church parking lot. She would swear her mother's jaw dropped a good six inches. "Madelyn? Is that you? I hardly recognized you."

"Oh, that's right," Maddie answered casually, as though her nerves hadn't been tied up in knots while she waited for her mother's reaction. "You haven't seen me since my trip to New York. I did the whole makeover thing—hair, clothes, the works."

"You look lovely." She circled Maddie, taking in the whole effect. "Really elegant. I've never seen you look better—" She stopped and frowned. "Oh Madelyn, what were you thinking? Heels? On a woman your size?"

Maddie could hear Dan's voice as clearly as if he stood behind her. It's time to make peace with who you are.

"Absolutely," she assured her mother with a wink. "It's a power thing."

After church, Maddie and her mother joined her sister and family at their house for lunch. Jennifer was a marvel. She could whip up a gourmet meal for six with the ease others had for making peanut butter sandwiches. After they'd eaten and the kids had been put down for naps and her brother-in-law had headed to the hospital for rounds, Maddie and her mother and Jennifer gathered around the dining-room table over cups of coffee.

"Well, glamorous baby sister, do you have any more surprises to spring on us?"

"No."

"Don't be modest, Madelyn. You haven't told your sister about your date to the reunion."

"It's true. I have a date." And because it wasn't Dan, Maddie couldn't muster much enthusiasm. "His name is—"

"—Colton Hartley. And he's a hunk," her mother finished for her. "As soon as Madelyn told me his name I called Jack's wife to get the details. You know how hard it is to get anything out of Madelyn."

Jennifer shot Maddie an amused look that said, "Or how hard it is for Maddie to get a word in edgewise."

"Is he nice?" Jennifer asked.

Maddie shrugged. "Yeah, I guess so—"

"He's charming," her mother supplied. "Jack's wife warned me to be prepared to be bowled over. She says he's smart, talented and fabulous looking. And our Madelyn has a date with him."

Maddie put down her cup and spoke the words that seemed to hang in the air after her mother's speech. "Will wonders ever cease?"

* * *

When it was time for Maddie to leave, Jennifer walked her to the door. "It's not true you know."

Maddie paused to look down at her. "What's not true?"

"That it's a wonder you have a date with Mr. Hunk. The only thing that surprises me is why it took so long for someone to appreciate you."

Maddie felt her face heat at the unexpected compliment. "You have to say that. You're my sister."

"Being your sister doesn't make me blind. I've known all along that you were lovely. Remember when Dad used to call you his treasure? He was right. You are a treasure. The problem was that you never believed it."

Jennifer reached up to brush back a lock of Maddie's hair. "You've changed. It's not just the clothes and hair. Somebody's finally convinced you to believe in yourself. I assume it's the Hunk mother was raving about. If he's smart enough to appreciate you, then I hope you fall madly in love with each other and live happily ever after. He's probably already in love with you."

Maddie snorted.

"Don't give me that. Remember, I know you. How could anybody not love you?"

Maddie cried all the way home.

Not the bitter racking sobs of a woman who'd lost at love but the slow hot tears of resigned acceptance. Time to deal with reality.

Dan didn't love her. Never had. While she was weaving fantasies of forever, he was planning a getaway. He'd sounded so relieved when she'd told him Colton had offered to take her to the reunion. As if he were glad to get her off his hands.

They were friends. If she were honest with herself she'd realize he'd never led her to believe anything else. Being a chronically nice guy, he liked to help her out when he could. Like taking her to New York to polish off some of the rough edges. Or offering to escort her to a family re-union if she couldn't find anyone else. He'd have done the same thing for anyone.

She'd been foolish to read more into the relationship. Blame it on inexperience or a desperate need to be loved, but she thought the flattering attention he showered on her and the stirring kisses had meant he was falling for her. He probably felt sorry for her.

Maddie shed a bathtub of tears on the long trip home. She ran through the purse pack of tissues she kept in her tote bag and had moved on to the roll of paper towels she kept stuffed under her front seat for emergencies.

She pulled into the parking garage at her apartment, found her spot and switched off the ignition. She flipped down the vanity mirror and gave herself a good hard look. Not a pretty sight. She was a red-eyed, tear-streaked mess.

Worse, she was a romantic idiot. She didn't even have the luxury of saying Dan had broken her heart. He'd never said she was anything but a friend. She was the one who'd lost sight of reality. She'd broken her own heart. How piti-ful was that?

So where did she go from here? However appealing, mourning to death wasn't a good option.

Maddie wiped away the last of the tears, wishing she had her dad to talk to. She closed her eyes and tried to imagine what he would say if he were there.

First thing he'd do would be to wrap her in a bear hug.

Her dad had been good at hugs. She could sure use one right about now. Next, he'd tell her to look at this positively. What did she have to work with? She thought about the question for a minute, as though he were sitting in the car beside her, waiting for an answer.

She had a five-foot-eleven-inch body she was stuck with, for better or for worse. A painful zing shot through her heart as she remembered the way Dan's eyes had glazed over when he saw her in the little robe.

She had a terrific new hairdo that made her feel feminine and ten pounds lighter. She had a new "body-conscious" wardrobe courtesy of Valkyrie, and several more garments speeding their way to Texas by Federal Express. She had three gorgeous new pairs of shoes. And she had a date to the reunion with Colton Hartley.

She could almost hear her dad urging her on. "Work with what you've got," he'd say. "Everybody falls. What makes the difference is whether you get up."

Maddie raised her chin. She was down, but not out. Wounded, but wiser. She climbed out of her car with a new resolve.

Dan had been good for her. She would be content with that. He didn't love her, but he'd taught her to love herself. It had been a hard lesson, but one she was determined never to forget.

If she went on loving him—and how could she not—then she'd do it privately. She was determined that no one would find out what a fool she'd been. And no one would ever know how much she hurt.

"Maddie? You got a minute?" Jack called from his office as she walked past.

She stopped and peeked inside. "Do you need something?"

"I'd like to talk to you."

She recognized that tone of voice. It meant if you don't have time, make it. "Sure."

"Come in. And close the door."

Uh-oh. Maddie pushed the door closed behind her and took the seat across the desk from him. She tried for a casual smile. "What can I do for you?"

"You can tell me how things are going."

Whew. All he wanted was an account update. Her face relaxed into a genuine smile. "Really great. PJ is thrilled with his new commercials. He says he gets several calls a day complimenting him on Electronic Era's new look."

Jack nodded. "He called me, too. Says you and Colton are responsible for turning business around."

"That's a bit of an exaggeration, but I'm glad he thinks so. Our meeting with Swanson Shoes went well. Paul just gave us final approval on the print ads. We'll start production next week."

"Excellent."

"Overall, I'd say business is great."

"I'm very proud of you. You've exceeded all of my highest expectations. But I don't want to talk about business right now." He sat back in his chair and studied her over the top of his steepled fingers. "I want to talk about you."

She tried not to squirm under his penetrating scrutiny. "Oh. There's really not much to say. I'm fine."

"That was succinct. Unfortunately, it tells me nothing."

She wasn't about to volunteer any information and inadvertently reveal her broken heart. "What would you like to know?"

"I'd like to know why you've been walking around here all week looking like you've lost your best friend."

She frowned. "I didn't realize I had."

He sat forward. "It's not obvious. In fact, to people who haven't watched you grow up, you probably look like happiness personified. The big smiles. The happy chatter. Running six directions at once. Only someone who knows you as well as I do would see that the look in your eyes doesn't match your actions."

She tried to shrug it off. "I don't know what you mean."

"I haven't seen your friend Dan this week."

She pinned a smile on her face. "He's out of town."

"I see. Maybe that accounts for the sadness I see."

"I'm not sad, Jack. He'll be back. Besides, we're just friends."

"That's not how it looked to me."

"It's true. Dan's such a nice guy, it's hard not to like him. But there's nothing more between us than friendship."

"Hmm." Jack seemed to digest that for a moment. "You prefer Colton to Dan?"

She didn't want to tell him the simple truth. That Colton was interested and Dan was not. "Colton's a nice guy."

"Word around the office is you two are seeing each other."

"Strictly business. Or at least it has been. I'm going out to dinner with him on Friday night, no big deal. And I'm taking him to the reunion, but only because he was available and I needed a date."

"I hope you have fun. As you said, Colton's a nice guy. But if you want my opinion, you can do better."

"Better than Colton?"

Jack nodded. "Don't get me wrong. I like him. I

wouldn't have hired him if I didn't think he was top-notch. He's the second-best person I've ever hired for Cue."

Maddie's brows shot up in question.

"You being the best," he said with a smile for clarification. "Colton's an excellent businessman. He's a natural in advertising. But I don't think he's good enough for you."

She didn't know where he was going with this. "We're not serious. Even if I was, I don't think Colton is the type to settle down with one woman. Not when there's fifty percent of the population waiting to be dazzled."

Jack laughed. "I should have trusted your good sense. Colton is a good-looking man. He turns a lot of heads. I was afraid that his biceps and pearly whites had affected your judgment. I know it's none of my business, but I would hate to see you married to a man who encouraged groupies. Larger than life is good for advertising, but lousy for a mate."

He stood and rounded the desk to place a hand on Maddie's shoulder. "I want you to be happy. You deserve the very best. I couldn't bear to see you settle for less."

Maddie met Colton at the Pines Restaurant at eight. It was common for a woman to meet her date at their destination, but that didn't mean she had to like it. She knew she was hopelessly tied to a previous century, but she wanted to be pursued.

She handed her car over to the valet and entered the lobby. She'd never been to the Pines before so she paused just inside the double doors to get her bearings.

The first person she noticed was Colton. He was standing at the reservations podium, his golden head tilted down to hear what the gorgeous little blond hostess was saying. From this distance Maddie couldn't read lips, but the blonde's body language said, "Come and get it."

Even in the shadows Maddie could see the answering "hubba hubba" in Colton's eyes. Fish gotta swim, birds gotta fly. Colton would flirt till the day that he died.

Maddie hummed the old song to herself as she approached Colton.

"Hi, Maddie. I didn't know you were here." He favored her with a lavish smile complete with dimples. "My date is here, Laura." He was already on a first-name basis with the hostess. "We're ready to be seated when you have a chance."

Laura shot Maddie a look that was equal parts malice and envy before leading them to a small round table toward the back of the room. Maddie couldn't resist sending her a smug grin that said, "Eat your heart out because he's all mine."

Maddie waited a second for Colton to get her chair. When he sat first, she figured she was on her own.

"It was great talking to you, Colton," Laura said as she handed them their menus. "Enjoy your meal."

"She seemed nice," Colton said, craning his neck to watch her wiggle back to her post.

"You have an inordinate talent for finding awfully nice people," Maddie said with a wry grin.

"You're right. I met you, didn't I?" He hit her with his slow-melt look. "Have I told you that you look terrific tonight?"

Whoa. Major compliment coming from the lips of perfection. So why didn't she feel flattered? Probably because the smooth phrase sounded too smooth. She wondered how many people he'd used that line on. Probably a dozen. Today.

Colton opened his menu. "I'm starved. We put in a full week this week. I think that entitles us to blow the diet. I'm thinking dinner *and* dessert."

She'd believe it when she saw it. "What's good?"

"Everything. I recommend the portobello mushroom and pasta. It's delicious and low-fat so it won't shoot your cholesterol to the moon."

How could she order a twelve-ounce steak with all the trimmings and a loaded baked potato in the company of a man with an encyclopedic knowledge of calories and fat grams?

"Sounds good."

Over salads and entrees they talked. About work, people they knew and the movies. The conversation seemed to confirm her previous observations about Colton. He was interested in money—both making it and spending it—maintaining his perfect body, and dating beautiful women. Her relatives would be totally impressed. Wasn't that what she wanted?

It turned out that the portobello pasta thing was delicious although Maddie thought the portions were on the skimpy side. A nice piece of chocolate cake would go a long way toward filling the empty spaces.

"I don't know about you," Colton said, "but I couldn't eat another bite. "Don't let me stop you. I promised dessert so feel free to order some."

No way. Not when he put it like that. It'd be like stamping the word *pig* across her forehead. "Thanks, no. A cup of coffee is fine."

More inconsequential chatter carried them through coffee and the check. Colton was fun to talk to. He seemed knowledgeable about a wide range of topics and he had a good sense of humor. Maddie didn't know why the conversation felt flat.

Maybe because over the two weeks of enforced togetherness they still had never gotten below the surface. She wasn't looking for intellectual exercise or deep philosophical discussion, but it would have been nice to get a glimpse of the real Colton.

She wanted to see beyond the superficialities of perfect skin and bones to the man inside. And it would have been nice to know he was interested enough in Maddie to want to see beyond her new hairstyle and clothes.

The few times she'd asked questions to stimulate a deeper discussion he'd answered glibly. The possibility had occurred to her more than once that his beautiful outside was all there was. She didn't know why that should depress her. He didn't have depth, but he was gorgeous. Wasn't that what she wanted? A beautiful man to prove to her family she wasn't a loser?

Maddie was suddenly sickeningly aware that her own motives didn't bear close scrutiny. Colton was interested in her because she was attractive. She was determined to land him as a date because he was attractive. Yuck. She was as shallow as Colton.

"Did you notice the way people looked at us in there?" Colton asked as they walked out to the parking lot.

"No," she said.

"We turned a lot of heads. It must be the height thing. We make a striking couple, Maddie. We'll knock 'em dead at the reunion tomorrow."

Ugh. To hear him spouting her agenda was the last straw. She didn't need to knock anyone dead at the reunion.

She was good enough without having a handsome ornament at her side to give her value.

She stopped and placed a hand on his arm. "Have you got a minute? I'd like to talk to you about the reunion."

Chapter Sixteen

Dan walked out of his darkroom in disgust. Fourteen rolls of film and not one photograph worth saving. No doubt about it, he was losing his touch.

He slumped into his chair and pulled a stack of eight-by-tens out of the top drawer of his desk. He laid them out, side by side into two rows and sighed.

The top five pictures he'd taken of Maddie at her apartment the night she'd fixed him dinner. The bottom five he'd taken on their trip to New York City. Arranged on his desk this way it looked like one of those before-and-after layouts magazines liked to do. However, unlike the models in the magazines, Maddie was beautiful both before and after.

There was no denying the post-makeover shots showed Maddie to best advantage. He studied the bottom row, pictures of Maddie strolling down the sidewalk in New York.

The new hairstyle, makeup and clothes played up her considerable assets to the hilt. Just thinking about her assets made Dan's stomach clench.

But she'd been beautiful all along. The intelligent sparkle in her eyes, the curve of her mouth and the warmth of her smile attracted him like a lost ship to a beacon of light.

He almost wished he'd left her in the before stage where he could keep her beauty all to himself. The stage where bushy eyebrows, baggy dresses and badger hair kept people like Colton away.

Then he thought of how happy she was now, how confident she appeared, and realized if he had to do it all over he'd do the same thing.

At least one of them was happy.

He looked up as he heard someone turn the doorknob. The door swung open slowly and Maddie peeked around the edge. "You're here!"

She looked good. Really good. He stood and shoved his hands in his pockets. "Yeah. Hi."

She walked toward the desk. "When did you get back?"

"A couple of days ago."

She stopped. "You didn't call."

"No."

Her face fell. "You didn't want to see me."

"It's not that."

"It's okay. I understand—" She glanced down at the pictures spread across his desk. "What are those?"

"Pictures of you."

"Yes, I can see that. What are you doing with them?"

"Torturing myself."

She tilted her head to see them better. "Are they that bad?"

His heart turned over when he saw all her old insecurities wash across her face. "No, Maddie. They are that good."

"So why are they torture?"

How could he describe what he was feeling? Just being in the same room with her was breaking his heart. "It's like seeing your very favorite dessert on the menu and being on a diet."

Her voice was barely a whisper. "Do you *want* to be on a diet?"

"No, ma'am."

Tears glistened in her eyes. "Then I think you'd better kiss me."

He did. He came out from behind the desk and was at her side in a heartbeat. She went warm and willing into his arms. Heat flared. Breathless and half crazy with desire he pulled away when he felt moisture on her cheeks.

"What's the matter?"

"I'm so happy."

"Aw, honey." He dug in his back pocket for the clean handkerchief he'd started carrying since their trip to New York. "Don't cry," he said, mopping up the tears. "You'll mess up your pretty dress."

She took the handkerchief from him to finish the job. "Thanks."

Suddenly aware of the time, Dan said, "It's after eleven. Have you been up here working all night?"

"No, I just drove over to look for you. I was out with Colton."

Her words hit him like a wave of ice-cold water. He took a step back and buried his hands in his pockets. "Oh."

"Why do you do that every time Colton's name comes up?"

"Do what?"

"Get stiff and formal."

She really didn't understand. "Think about it, Maddie. He's got you. I don't. I'm jealous."

"Of Colton? That's ridiculous."

"Don't tell that to his thousands of adoring fans."

"They only act that way because they don't know him as well as I do."

Jealousy shafted through him. "And just how well *do* you know him?"

"Well enough to know he doesn't make me feel like I do when I'm with you."

He cradled her face in his hands. "How do you feel with me?"

"Powerful. Beautiful. Special. When I'm with you I want to be the best person I can be. When I'm with Colton I feel as though I never measure up."

Dan frowned. "That sounds like two sides of the same coin."

"It's not. You're comfortable. Colton's not."

He dropped his hands. "And I'm supposed to be flattered by that?"

"No. You're supposed to kiss me."

He did, though softer and gentler this time.

"Mmm," Maddie said, laying her head against his shoulder. "I've been dreaming of this."

Hope constricted his chest. "If I didn't know better, I'd think you sounded like a woman in love."

Maddie stepped back from the circle of his arms to study his face. Dan's breath locked in his throat as he waited for her to speak.

Her dark eyes softened and her mouth curved upward

as she said, "Oh, I'm a woman in love, all right. You just haven't been around for me to tell you."

Dan's breath whooshed out in a joyous rush. She loved him!

He pulled her close, raining kisses over her face before throwing his head back and laughing with delight. Maddie loved him. It was almost too good to believe except for the fact that she was here, in his arms, as warm, living proof.

She loved him. How was it possible? She'd been so focused on Colton, Dan had hardly dared to dream she'd see past all that golden perfection to him, the man that truly loved her.

And he did love her. Dan knew she'd captured his heart the moment he'd caught her in his arms the first time they'd met. He'd come to believe Maddie was the reason he'd returned to Texas. She was what had been missing in his life. Maddie was the beauty he'd been searching for.

He lowered his mouth to hers. The kiss began tenderly, as a celebration of the miracle of love they'd found, then slowly heated with the passion of two people giving themselves wholly to one another.

Breathlessly he said, "I'm glad I cut my trip short."

"Me, too," Maddie murmured against his shoulder. She lifted her head. "I almost forgot to ask. How was your trip?"

"Terrible. I took lots of pictures, but I never found what I was looking for. And I couldn't find anything beautiful."

She brushed a strand of hair from his forehead. "You've been working too hard. Maybe you just need a break."

"Maybe I need to take you with me so I'll have beauty wherever I go."

Maddie sighed. "That's so nice."

He shook his head. "I told you before. I'm not nice. I'm just crazy about you. I love you, Maddie."

She smiled up at him. "I love you, too."

"Your reunion is tomorrow isn't it?"

"Yeah, why?"

He frowned. "Don't you think it's going to be a bit awkward taking Colton when you're in love with me?"

She shrugged. "I'm not taking him."

"But—"

"I told him I didn't need an escort after all."

Dan's grin split his face. "Poor guy. I'd say you broke his heart if I thought he had one."

Maddie wagged a finger at him. "Be nice. He's still my partner."

Since she loved him, not Colton, he could afford to be magnanimous. "That's fine, but no more Dynamic Duo. If you're going to be paired with anybody, I want it to be with me."

"Does that mean you'll take me to the reunion?"

He grinned. "I thought you'd never ask."

Maddie and Dan arrived when the reunion was in full swing. Dan parked his truck in the last open space next to the balloon-festooned pavilion.

He switched off the engine and leaned across the seat to squeeze Maddie's hand. "Have I told you today that you look amazing?"

She smiled at the sweetness of knowing he'd meant it every time he said it. "Only about half a dozen times."

For someone who ordinarily dreaded reunions the way others dreaded a trip to the dentist, Maddie *felt* amazing. She was primed to handle anything her relatives could dish out.

The new sundress was a definite ego boost, but it had been Dan's starry-eyed look when he picked her up that morning that had supercharged her. He thought she was wonderful. Nothing else mattered.

They climbed out of the car and walked hand-in-hand toward the crowded picnic tables.

"Incoming relative at two o'clock," Dan muttered under his breath.

Maddie glanced over to see her mother closing in fast.

"Madelyn, you finally made it." After a quick hug she turned to Dan, "And this must be Colton." Her mother flashed him an appreciative grin. "I can see all the rumors about you are true."

Maddie's voice was strangled. "Mom, this is Dan."

Dan's smile was a mile wide as he extended a hand to her mother. "Colton was last week. It was touch and go for a while, but I'm happy to say I beat him out for your daughter's affections. It's great to meet you. Maddie has told me so much about you."

Her mother looked genuinely shocked. "Oh, Dan, I'm so sorry."

"No problem. I bet it's a real challenge to keep up with all Maddie's men."

Maddie could see her mother studying her with new eyes. "Yes," she said, her voice filled with wonder, "Our Maddie is full of surprises."

Her mother seemed suddenly to remember her manners. "Why don't you two come with me? I'll introduce Dan to everyone."

"In a minute, Mom. We want to get something to drink first."

"Fine, dear. You two have fun. I'll catch up with you

later." Her mother took off at a fast trot, nearly upsetting old Uncle Clyde and his loaded paper plate in her hurry to get to Maddie's sister and relay this new incredible information.

"Now look what you've done," Maddie scolded Dan as they watched her mother's back disappear into the crowd. "You've convinced her that I'm a femme fatale. 'All Maddie's men.' Where do you come up with this stuff?"

He shrugged while trying unsuccessfully to mask his grin. "It just came to me."

On their way to the refreshments table for a couple of Aunt Jane's famous freshly squeezed lemonades, Maddie and Dan were waylaid by a distant cousin recruiting contenders for the three-legged race.

"It really wouldn't be a reunion without one three-legged race," Dan said to Maddie.

"Fine," she said with a tolerant roll of her eyes. "One race."

They took their places in the freshly mowed field, inside legs tied together with a short piece of rope, and waited for the whistle to start them. Maddie and Dan were a shoe-in. With their long-legged strides they covered the short course in a hurry, leaving her smaller relatives in the dust.

Uncle Bob presided over the awards distribution at the finish line. "Maddie and Dan are the winners," he declared to the group before presenting them with the prize—two tickets to the movies. "Outstanding teamwork."

Dan dropped a quick kiss on Maddie's lips before whispering, "Don't let anybody kid you, size matters."

He was kind enough to give piggyback rides to several squealing cousins and second cousins before Maddie dragged him away to a shady spot in the pavilion to rest. They sipped ice-cold lemonade and watched the activities.

Dan sat on the picnic bench, his back resting against the table and his long legs stretched out in front of him. "Having fun?"

"Yeah, I really am. Can you believe it?" It was true. She *was* having fun. It made all the difference to be there with him. She took his hand and said, "I'm glad you're here."

He lifted her hand to his mouth for a kiss. "You couldn't have kept me away."

Little by little the tables under the pavilion filled as families came in out of the sun. Aunt Linda, Maddie's mother's terminally organized sister who coordinated the reunion every year, led the group in songs and hymns as had become the family tradition. While they sang, the rest of the family straggled in.

After a particularly moving rendition of "Amazing Grace," Aunt Linda took the floor for the annual state-of-the-family address. In it she acknowledged the families present and invited each to stand up and share news about kids or jobs or whatever.

Maddie hadn't expected to be included in the address.

"Maddie," Aunt Linda said as she looked out over the crowd, "I see you've brought a friend with you. Son, why don't you stand up and introduce yourself?"

Maddie flashed Dan a look of apology.

Dan stood to a nice welcoming round of applause. "I'm Dan Willis. I'm a photographer in Fort Worth."

"Nice to have you, Dan. How did you meet our Maddie?"

"I met her in the cafeteria at work. Just one look at her and I was hooked. She's so beautiful she knocked me off my feet. And I don't think I'm putting words in her mouth when I say Maddie fell for me the first time we met."

Maddie and Dan shared a smile at the memory of their near-cataclysmic first meeting.

Aunt Linda, reunion coordinator and family historian, must have sensed a scoop. "That sounds serious."

"Boy, I hope so. I guess now's as good a time as any to find out." Dan reached out to take Maddie's hand. "Maddie, I love you. I need your beauty in my life, today and every day. Will you marry me?"

A startled hush fell over the room as all eyes zeroed in on Maddie and Dan, waiting for her reply.

The question caught Maddie off guard. Why would a private man like Dan propose marriage to her in front of a room full of relatives? As her gaze flew to his seeking an answer, he winked, and she knew in that instant he'd done it for her.

By pledging his love to her in front of them, he was affirming her. He was telling her family that she was beautiful and worthy of love.

She felt emotion swell in her heart until her chest hurt. What kind of man would do that for her?

She smiled. The man she would love every day of her life. "Yes, Dan, I'll marry you."

* * * * *

Bestselling fantasy author Mercedes Lackey turns traditional fairy tales on their heads in the land of the Five Hundred Kingdoms.

Elena, a Cinderella in the making, gets an unexpected chance to be a Fairy Godmother. But being a Fairy Godmother is hard work and she gets into trouble by changing a prince who is destined to save the kingdom, into a donkey—but he really deserved it!

Can she get things right and save the kingdom?
Or will her stubborn desire to teach this ass
of a prince a lesson get in the way?

On sale November 2004.
Visit your local bookseller.

Coming in December 2004

SILHOUETTE *Romance* ®

presents a brand-new book from
reader favorite

Linda Goodnight

Don't miss...

THE LEAST LIKELY GROOM, #1747

Injured rodeo rider Jett Garret meets his match in feisty
nurse Becka Washburn who only wants to tend to his
wounds and send him on his way. But after some intensive
at-home care, the pretty single mom realizes that this
Texas cowboy is slowly working his way
into her heart.

Available at your favorite retail outlet.

If you enjoyed what you just read,
then we've got an offer you can't resist!

Take 2 bestselling love stories FREE!

Plus get a FREE surprise gift!

Clip this page and mail it to Silhouette Reader Service™

IN U.S.A.
3010 Walden Ave.
P.O. Box 1867
Buffalo, N.Y. 14240-1867

IN CANADA
P.O. Box 609
Fort Erie, Ontario
L2A 5X3

YES! Please send me 2 free Silhouette Romance® novels and my free surprise gift. After receiving them, if I don't wish to receive anymore, I can return the shipping statement marked cancel. If I don't cancel, I will receive 4 brand-new novels every month, before they're available in stores! In the U.S.A., bill me at the bargain price of $3.57 plus 25¢ shipping and handling per book and applicable sales tax, if any*. In Canada, bill me at the bargain price of $4.05 plus 25¢ shipping and handling per book and applicable taxes**. That's the complete price and a savings of at least 10% off the cover prices—what a great deal! I understand that accepting the 2 free books and gift places me under no obligation ever to buy any books. I can always return a shipment and cancel at any time. Even if I never buy another book from Silhouette, the 2 free books and gift are mine to keep forever.

210 SDN DZ7L
310 SDN DZ7M

Name	(PLEASE PRINT)	
Address	Apt.#	
City	State/Prov.	Zip/Postal Code

Not valid to current Silhouette Romance® subscribers.

Want to try two free books from another series?
Call 1-800-873-8635 or visit www.morefreebooks.com.

* Terms and prices subject to change without notice. Sales tax applicable in N.Y.
** Canadian residents will be charged applicable provincial taxes and GST.
  All orders subject to approval. Offer limited to one per household.
  ® are registered trademarks owned and used by the trademark owner and or its licensee.

SROM04R   ©2004 Harlequin Enterprises Limited

SILHOUETTE *Romance*®

In a
Fairy Tale
World

Six reluctant couples.
Five classic love stories.
One matchmaking princess.
And time is running out!

Don't miss a moment of this enchanting miniseries from Silhouette Romance.

Their Little Cowgirl by MYRNA MACKENZIE
Silhouette Romance #1738

Rich Man, Poor Bride by LINDA GOODNIGHT
Silhouette Romance #1742
Available November 2004

Her Frog Prince by SHIRLEY JUMP
Silhouette Romance #1746
Available December 2004

Engaged to the Sheik by SUE SWIFT
Silhouette Romance #1750
Available January 2005

Nighttime Sweethearts by CARA COLTER
Silhouette Romance #1754
Available February 2005

Twice a Princess by SUSAN MEIER
Silhouette Romance #1758
Available March 2005

Only from Silhouette Books!

SILHOUETTE *Romance*

COMING NEXT MONTH

#1746 HER FROG PRINCE—Shirley Jump
In a Fairy Tale World...
Bradford Smith needed to get rid of his scruffy image...
fast! And buying a week of feisty beauty Parris Hammond's
consulting services was the answer to his prayers. But would
the sassy socialite be able to turn this sexy, but stylistically chal-
lenged dud into the stud of her dreams?

#1747 THE LEAST LIKELY GROOM—Linda Goodnight
Clinging to a dream, injured bull rider Jett Garret would do *anything* to return to the circuit—and the pretty nurse he'd
hired was his ticket back to the danger he craved. But after
spending time with Becka Washburn and her young son,
Jett soon found himself thinking the real danger might
be losing this ready-made family.

**#1748 THE TRUTH ABOUT PLAIN JANE—
Roxann Delaney**
In a big curly wig and fake glasses, Meg Chastain had come to
Trey Brannigan's dude ranch to write the exposé that would
make her career. Meg knew the Triple B meant everything
to Trey...but she was out to prove that she could be
so much more....

#1749 LOVE CHRONICLES—Lissa Manley
Sunny Williams was on a mission—to convince oh-so-sexy
Connor Forbes that her holistic methods would enhance his
small-town medical practice. The dishy doctor had never
valued alternative medicine, but as Connor spent time with
the beautiful blonde, he began to discover that he might
want to make sweet Sunny his partner for good!

SRCNM1104